FIRESHIP

They plugged Michael Yarrow into the new ETHANAC computer to see what would happen before they used it on someone important. It was meant to enhance a secret agent's abilities to penetrate any computer, military or civilian, anywhere—but if it had hidden dangers, better to use up an insignificant lab technician than a trained agent. . . .

When the amiable but not-too-bright Yarrow was connected to ETHANAC, his mind was flooded and expanded almost intolerably—that was what the planner had expected.

What they hadn't counted on was that ETHANAC could discover new horizons, too. . . .

MOTHER AND CHILD

The king's men left Etaa's husband, Hywel the smith, smashed on the rocks below the cliffs and bore her to their master's bed. The Neaane were the masters of their world, their power supported by the living Gods who walked among them, and they feared no reprisal from the despised Kotaane. But suddenly there were raids, and fire and death in the night . . . and the Kotaane were led by a gaunt, maimed figure known as the Smith. Only the Gods could save the Neaane—but the Gods had turned against them.

The Latest Science Fiction and Fantasy From Dell Books

FIRESHIP

Joan D. Vinge

A DELL BOOK

Published by
Dell Publishing Co., Inc.
1 Dag Hammarskjold Plaza
New York, New York 10017

"Fireship" originally appeared in
Analog Science Fiction/Science Fact Magazine,
December 1978 issue.

"Mother and Child" originally appeared in
ORBIT 16, edited by Damon Knight
and published by Harper & Row, Publishers, Inc. (1975).

Dell ® TM 681510, Dell Publishing Co., Inc.

ISBN: 0-440-15794-3

Printed in the United States of America

First printing—December 1978

FIRESHIP

I really must have been drunk. Because boy, was I ever hung over. . . . I woke up groaning out of a dream that I'd just had my head shrunk, and couldn't tell if it'd been a dream or not. I dragged my face up off the pillow, trying to see the clock on the bedside bar . . . the clocks, there were two of 'em. Funny, I only remembered one, last night. *Ohh. Last night—*

But what'd finally got me awake wasn't just the ringing in my ears: the viewphone was starting into "Starlight Serenade" for about the tenth time. Finally remembering where I was, sort of, I crawled back across the bed's two meters of jelly to the phone on the other side. I took a look at myself in the mirrored screen. And then I hit BLANK SCREEN, before I pressed the VOICE button. "Hello?" I said. It sounded like, "Huh."

"Mr. Ring? Are you there? This is the lobby—" She was pretty, but she had a voice like disaster sirens.

I considered maybe dying, and mumbled something.

She looked relieved. "Visitors to see you, Mr. Ring."

Confused warnings went off down in my mind: "Are they wearin' uniforms?" It's nice to be wanted, but not by the U.S. government.

"No, they're not, sir." She blinked at me. "Shall I send them up?"

"Ugh, no—" I waited for my head to fall off; no

luck. "Uh, jus' tell 'em I'll be down, soon." *Give or take a couple of hours. . . .*

"All right. Thank you, Mr. Ring." The screen went blank, but her smile stayed behind. I wondered what she did in her spare time. I'd have to ask her, if I lived long enough. I lay back on the blue satin sheets, trying to decide whether to sit up or give up.

Sitting up won, and I pushed my feet over the edge of the bed onto the floor. They came down in a pile of cold hard slippery things. I pulled myself up and leaned forward–

"Oh, geez–not again." The floor around the bed was ankle-deep in money. Or in chips from the Hotel Xanadu's casino, which was pretty much the same thing. And I couldn't remember anything about last night. They'd done it to me again, Ring and that computer–gotten me so stinking drunk I was putty in their hands: Michael Yarrow, the all-day sucker. "Why do I put up with this?" I pressed my hands against my head, having answered my own stupid question. *Because you need them.* Besides, I couldn't blame Ring; if I was blind drunk last night, so was he . . . except he was supposed to be in charge, and he'd let ETHANAC take over. "You promised, you promised you wouldn't do this t' me again! What if somebody noticed–"

But they weren't even listening; I wasn't plugged in. If I was gonna yell at myself, I might as well have an audience. Not that they'd listen; I was just the body around here. . . . *Oh, knock off the self-pity; plug in and you'll feel better.*

I fumbled around in the chips until I found the cord that was attached to ETHANAC's breadloaf-sized case on the floor beside the bed. I pulled the cord up and stuck it into the socket low on my spine, felt the electric flow of the change start and spread, turning all my nerve endings into stars. . . .

I stretched and shook my head until the static cleared, finishing Yarrow's almost obscene sigh of pleasure for him. The mental rat's nest of his hangover mercifully cleared out with the static, for which I was supremely grateful; even though there wasn't much we could do for his body: his bloodshot baby blues stared back at me forlornly from the phone mirror, half obscured by rumpled brown hair, in a face the color of oatmeal. I don't like oatmeal. I looked away, grimacing, feeling Yarrow's indignation at his betrayal push up through my control again; I hate those mornings when I can't seem to wake up— *Damn it, is that any way to treat the body that's gotta carry you around?* . . . BE A SPORT, MICHAEL—even ETHANAC was butting in, flushed with his triumph at the gaming tables—LET YOURSELF ENJOY LIFE ONCE IN A WHILE. . . . *Enjoy life? Gettin' your own mind totally wiped, and then takin' advantage of it, ain't my idea of a good time.* . . . ALL RIGHT, I KNOW IT TOOK TEN OR TWELVE DRINKS TO BREAK DOWN YOUR INHIBITIONS. BUT WASN'T IT WORTH IT—?

I looked down again at the pile of chips around my feet, and felt a gloating recapitulation of last night's gambling spree overload my consciousness. I frowned, disgusted, and let Yarrow go on complaining for both of us. *Tryin' to break the bank, on neutral ground! Where anybody could've seen it, an' be half a million U.S. bucks richer for turning me in, by now! My God. I mean, just who the hell is waiting for us downstairs right now?* . . . DON'T CAUSE YOURSELF UNNECESSARY DISTRESS. IF HEW KNEW YOU WERE HERE, THEY WOULD SIMPLY KICK IN THE DOOR AND DRAG YOU AWAY. . . .

. . . . *Why am I arguing with myself?* I reasserted and reintegrated, getting rid of the aggravating schizo conversations. Leaning forward, I drew the drapes and let in some daylight. Clouding over, just as predicted: This was the Day of the Rain. I squinted out at the brick red Martian sky patterning with oppressive mud-colored clouds, and decided that if HEW ever caught up with me I'd have only myself to blame . . . me, myself, and I. *We are not amused.* Yarrow's hand picked up ETHANAC's suitcase obligingly: I stumbled off to the bathroom to make myself fit for human company.

"In Xanadu"—according to Samuel Taylor Coleridge—"did Kublai Khan a stately pleasure-dome decree, where Alph, the sacred river, ran through caverns measureless to man, down to a sunless sea." The original may have existed only in Coleridge's opium dreams, but here on Mars the dream has come true, thanks to the limitless funds and the boundless ego of Khorram Kabir. What dread secrets do Khorram Kabir and Kublai Khan share? The same initials, for one thing. . . . But Kabir didn't want the comparison to end there. Being the eccentric head of a multinational, multibillion-dollar financial empire, you could say he qualified as an emperor. But he wanted his own Xanadu; and like a true twenty-first-century mogul, he created one—and made certain it would pay.

Hence, the Xanadu, the pleasure dome extraordinary: luxury hotel, resort, spa—and gambling casino. The old me had never been a gambler, because I was just smart enough to realize what I was really bad at. The new me, I'd just discovered, was a little too smart for my own good. I'd actually believed—and maybe it was true—that I'd only come here to watch the rain. I'd been on Mars for nearly an Earth year, but because of my peculiar status I'd never had the nerve to visit the Tourist Belt before. But the whole reason I'd ended up on Mars in the first place was the simple desire to see more of the world—any world. And for an entire year I'd been listening to the ecstatic accounts of how my various buddies in software maintenance had reduced their credit to zero in one glorious blowout at the Xanadu. And finally I couldn't stand it anymore—

But now, as I stepped out of the lift bubble at the lobby, my common sense was trying to tell me that I should just cut my vacation short, just pack up my money and steal silently back to the Arab territories. Except that someone was waiting to see me. I didn't know anyone here who'd *want* to see me, for any good reason; and yet my curiosity was tingling like a cat's. All my life I'd believed that someday some stranger would come up to me in a cafeteria and tell me that I was a long-lost heir, or in a subway station and tell me I'd won the National Lottery. Or in the Hotel Xanadu, and tell me I was under arrest . . . ?

In spite of that, I crossed the crowded lobby to the information center. The floor of the lobby, which is a good one hundred fifty meters across, is a hand-laid mosaic. Radiating out from the main desk are scenes of ancient Oriental splendor; it made me mildly uncomfortable to step on peoples' faces. But then, that was probably what the original Xanadu had been all about. . . . Behind me in the elevator shaft, drifting spheres of colored glass carried guests from one level to another through a fittingly tinted fall of golden water (water being worth more than gold here on Mars): Alph, the sacred river, rushing softly down to its sunless sea—in the depths of the Xanadu's casino levels in the Caves of Ice.

One of the young studs at the information counter came up to me, looking bored, tugging at his velvet bolero. "Help you, sir?"

"Ethan Ring. Someone was asking for me?" I tugged at my knee-length, wine-red velvet jacket, doing my best to match him ennui for ennui.

"I'll check, sir." No contest. He drifted away, and I turned to look out across the lobby, in case anyone seemed to be looking for me. No one did, as far as I could tell. The murmur of conversation flowed into the muted intricacies of chamber music by Bach, played by a live string quartet in the corner of the room—tasteful, if not entirely appropriate. Most of the wandering guests looked as self-consciously gaudy and overdressed as I did.

Beyond them the wall was a curving window, taking full advantage of the view, which is spectacular. The Xanadu is located on the choicest piece of real estate on all Mars—midway up the slope of Mt. Olympus. The hotel itself, which stretches twenty-five storeys up the side of the slope, is a parabolic hyperboloid (a form which reminded Yarrow of an apple core), so that every floor has an equal share of the view—of the endless subtle variations of russet and red and orange across the Martian plain; and the glassy, brassy sprawl of the freeport city that surrounds Elysian Field, and spreads up to the steep cliff-face at the volcano's foot.

"Mr. Ring?" The stud was back at last. "Are you the one who won fifty thousand seeyas last night?"

I looked at him. Fifty thousand International Credit Units . . . my God, that was almost three hundred thousand dollars! "Uh, yes, I suppose I am." Total disbelief is a good substitute for total disinterest, even on Yarrow's open, flexible face.

The stud looked at me with an expression which might have been awe, or might have been envy, but which at least was not boredom. "Oh. Your . . . ah, your party is waiting in the Peacock Lounge, sir."

"Thanks." So my visitors were having a hair of the dog that had bitten me, while they waited. . . . I crossed the lobby to the lounge. I paused inside the entrance, checking out the afternoon's clientele, with no idea at all of whom I was looking for. But then I saw her, sitting alone in a booth by the curving window and smiling at me; and I knew that if she wasn't the one I was looking for, then whoever it was could go to hell.

I went down the single step past the scrolled railing, and started across the vividly blue Persian carpet—seeing it all with a heightened awareness, as if this were the first and last moment of my life. But most of all, seeing her: The cascade of raven hair that lay across her shoulder like night's cloak; the dark, elvish eyes; the sea-green dress that bared one shoulder and draped the other like a wave, trailing crystal beads like a foaming crest from wrist to hemline. Last night in the casino, in the eerie black-light fluorescence of the Caves of Ice, that foam of glittering beads had been all the colors of the rainbow—

Last night she'd stood beside me while I played at the highstakes tables . . . and all the while ETHANAC had been too damn lost in high-rolling fever to even register her presence, that sodden fool Yarrow had been falling in love. And that meant. . . .

"I love you, Lady Luck," Yarrow blurted, before I could bite his tongue. "Everthing I have is yours."

She looked slightly taken aback, for which I couldn't blame her. "All fifty thousand seeyas of it?" she said.

I straightened up, wishing fervently that I could give myself a partial lobotomy. Yarrow's part. "Maybe I'd better go out and come in again."

"Consider it done." She smiled, this time. "Good afternoon, Ethan. Sit down. May I buy you a drink?"

I sat down across the small table from her, wanting to sit down beside her. "No drink, thanks. I think I reached the saturation point last night."

"At least you haven't forgotten me. . . ." She leaned on a slender fist, and the smile turned rueful. "I was beginning to think you'd stood me up."

"Forget you—?" At least she was the one who'd called; at least she'd wanted to see me again. I swore silently at the total blank where she should have been in ETHANAC's record of last night. "I'm just trying to figure out how I ever let you slip away."

"You drank a little too much of the Milk of

Paradise—I tucked you in myself." The smile turned more rueful yet; my backbone turned to jelly.

And I remembered the empty bed I'd come to in this afternoon; my hand closed dangerously over the case hooked onto my belt. "I'll make it up to you tonight."

"You already have."

"I have," I said; half afraid she'd tell me how.

"By winning fifty thousand seeyas. By winning at every game you played last night. . . ."

My face stiffened; it hadn't occurred to me that she was after my money. My ego shriveled. But infatuation is a blind beggar: if she wanted money, I could give it to her. . . . "I can do it every night, with you beside me, Lady Luck."

She raised her eyebrows. "You really mean that, don't you?"

"More than I've ever meant anything in my life."

Surprise, and an expression that might have been sorrow worried her face. "No, I mean, you literally mean that luck had nothing to do with it—that you could do it every night. Don't you, Michael Yarrow?"

My face went entirely blank, this time. I could feel all the expression drain away: Somebody had pulled the plug on me at last. Had I done it to myself? Had I really been so drunk and so careless that I'd told her my name was Michael Yarrow? But she'd called me *Ethan*. . . . I continued to look at her blankly. "Run that one by again?"

"You're a hustler, Michael Yarrow. You can calculate the odds with lightning speed when you gamble. The house doesn't stand a chance. And that's not all you can do: Your intelligence is artificially augmented by an ETHANAC 500 computer."

I shook my head. "Lady Luck, if I told you that last night, I apologize. It was only to augment my own ego. My real name is Ethan Ring, and I do software maintenance for the colonial government of the Arab States, here on Mars. And when I get drunk, not only am I a hustler, but I'm also a pathological liar."

"You're even better when you're sober." She reached out and took my hand, and turned it over as if she were reading my palm. "Nice try. But fingerprints don't lie; and yours belong to Michael Yarrow, U.S. citizen, who is wanted back on Earth for theft, sabotage, and high treason. The price on your head is five hundred thousand dollars." She looked up at me again, with deadly calm.

I knew now how Prince Charming must have felt when Cinderella turned into a scrubwoman. "All right." My hand turned into a fist, and I removed it from her grasp. "I have three hundred thousand dollars worth of chips up in my room. If you really know what I can do, you know I can get you twice the amount of that reward, and in half the time it would take the U.S. government to get it to you. Would a million dollars be sufficient to keep your mouth shut?"

Surprise again, feigned or real. "So you would be willing to embezzle seven hundred thousand dollars?"

I frowned. " 'Willing' is hardly the word. But yes, I'd do just about anything to avoid having my health ruined by the Department of Health, Education, and Welfare."

"I see. That does make it easier—" She glanced out the window at the sky, which was getting darker every minute, like my mood. "Unfortunately, I'm not really interested in money."

"But you're not a misguided patriot, either. So just what is it you're after?"

"Tell me—" she said, in total *non sequitur,* "why did you say that to me, when you first came in?"

I shrugged. "I never like to start out a relationship on the defensive. Tell *me* something: Did you put me up to the gambling last night?"

She shook her head; I tried not to watch the way it made her hair ripple and play with light. "No. You'd already won twenty thousand seeyas when I first noticed you. That's what made me curious. What I'm after, Yarrow—"

"Call me Ethan."

"—is your brain."

"Is that all. Shall I wrap it up, or will you dissect it here?"

She looked pained. "I'll ignore that. My name is Hanalore Takhashi." She pushed a small white business card toward me across the transparent tabletop.

I picked it up obediently, and read:

MEINE GEDANKEN SIND FREI.

" 'My thoughts are free'?" I glanced up. "From what I've heard, your thoughts are damned expensive." I recognized the motto of Free Thought, Incorporated, which as I well knew was a mercenary think-tank, renting the problem-solving brilliance of its employees to any business, organization, or government willing to meet its exorbitant fee. "So you're a fink, then?"

"We prefer the term 'information consultant.' " She tapped the stem of her wineglass. Somewhere back in the real world I heard a crash, as some barfly tossed off a drink and then the glass: An old custom, recently revived, like most things in dubious taste. "And the motto represents our philosophy, not our fee policy. We refuse to be limited, by either intimidation or questionable loyalties, to serving any one government or creed. That's why our organization is based here on Mars, even though we do most of our work for customers on Earth."

"Yes, I know; very noble." My brain began to function analytically again. "But, you mean you're simply trying to recruit me? Blackmail really isn't necessary—"

She shook her head. "Considering your problems with the American government, you wouldn't be of much use to us. I just want to borrow your special skills for one small, computer-oriented project. No more, no less. Cooperate with me, and I'll forget I ever saw you. Refuse, and—"

"And if I'm lucky, I won't live to regret it." Instant replay: some choice examples of some not-so-swift retributions that might occur when Uncle Sam's prodigal nephew returned home in disgrace. The Reduction to Component Parts of Ethan Ring would start with unplugging the cord from the socket in my spine, but it probably wouldn't end there. . . . Hanalore Takhashi leaned back against the peacock-blue leather of the booth, watching my paranoia show. Five minutes ago I'd been wondering where she'd been all my life; now I just wanted to know when she was going back. "Lady Luck, you really know how to screw a guy. And that's not a compliment. Just one little job, you said, and you'll go out of my life forever?" *You lose some; and you lose some.* A smile is a kind of grimace. I smiled. "It's a deal."

"Good." Her face relaxed, and I suddenly realized how tense she'd looked. "Shall we go, then?"

"Go?" I remained sitting. "Go where?"

"Outside. To meet someone." She waved a hand at the window, and nodded at the other guests, who were gradually wandering out of the bar. "The rain should be starting about fourteen-twenty. You don't want to miss it, do you?"

Rain on Mars is like snow in Southern California: it doesn't happen very often. When it does, it's like New Year's Eve—a grand excuse for lunacy and laughter and hugging total strangers. Computerized forecasting techniques and the comparative simple-mindedness of Martian weather make it possible to plan your celebrations in advance; so when storms pass over the Tourist Belt—over Olympus or Fat City or the Mariner Valley—the Martians jostle with the visiting Earthies for the chance to get their helmets wet, and the resort hotels make the most of it. . . . And this time I'd succumbed, like a thousand other homesick colonists, to: "The midnight that it sang you to sleep . . . the time it wrapped your hills in steel and silver . . . that afternoon in the park, when you watched it paint a triple rainbow in watercolors across the sky. . . . Remember the rain?"

And if I hadn't remembered it so painfully well, I wouldn't be in this spot. I got up glumly. "You're damn right I don't want to miss it."

We went back across the hotel lobby and rented candy-colored pressure suits at the tail of the shuffling crowd. We followed the rest of them into the airlock, a long downhill ramp that led out onto the Xanadu's "balcony"—a flagstoned terrace big enough for the Olympic Games. I noticed a few stalwarts had rented O_2 breathers and parkas instead of full suits, in order to get as close to the rain as humanly possible; I personally hadn't gotten that homesick yet. They claim a terraformed Mars is an improvement; and it is true that melting the polar caps has increased the atmospheric pressure enough that now anyone with six pairs of long underwear, an oxygen mask, and the constitution of a Sherpa can walk around outside without dying. But the climate is miserable, cold, and most of the time painfully dry—in other words, a lot like winter in my home town of Cleveland, Ohio. I consider that a dubious improvement.

We worked our way around the fringes of the gaudy crowd, the sound of their enthusiasm in my suit speakers nearly deafening me. At the point furthest from the airlock I saw two figures standing by the low stone fence, more or less alone. One of them raised a gloved hand as we approached; I wasn't sure whether he was waving at us, or checking for rain.

"Cephas? Basil? I've got him—" My rhetorical question was answered as we joined them in the corner of the terrace. Hanalore sat down on one branch of the corner bench; I sat on the other, while the two men looked at me speculatively. Behind the clear bubble of one helmet I saw the tallest black man I'd ever seen—probably the tallest man I'd ever seen—with a scholarly graying mustache and sideburns. He sat down next to Hanalore, as she slid toward the inner corner of the bench. And waiting for me to do the same, with a lack of enthusiasm clearly approaching my own, was the second man. A man who gave new meaning to the term "beak-nosed." In his patterned pressure suit, he made me think of the puffin in a book I'd had as a child. He might have made me nostalgic, under other circumstances. I slid over grudgingly, and he sat down.

"Would you mind setting that case on the ground?" The tone suggested that he didn't care whether I minded or not. He rapped on my plastic exoskeleton familiarly.

I checked the seal of the emergency equipment plug, where ETHANAC's cord passed through my suit. "Friend, you may not object to sitting on your brain; but no, I don't put mine on the floor."

It took a second for that to register, after which three pairs of eyes impaled me with varying degrees of censure. My friend the puffin said, "No. Absolutely not, Hana. I can't work with a man like that; we couldn't possibly trust him–" I urged him on mentally. "He's a criminal! We should report him to the Americans and let it go at that."

More like the urge to kill.

"Basil." Hana raised her voice over the general clamor in our helmets. "You can't blame him for being a little sharp." She lowered it again, "After all, we're blackmailing the man." She looked back at me. "These are my colleagues–Cephas Ntebe, and Basil Kraus."

Rhymes with "louse."

"Cephas, Basil, this is–" she glanced away.

"Michael Ethan Yarrow Ring," we said.

They looked confused. " 'What's in a name,' Yarrow?" Ntebe asked.

"As old What's-his-name once said." I sat back against the wall, looked over and down the long,

long slope to the sheer drop of the cliff at the volcano's foot. "Simply that I am not Michael Yarrow. I'm Ethan Ring."

"You just happen to live in someone else's body." Hana gestured sarcastically at my hidden fingerprints.

I nodded. "Exactly."

"This man is impossible!" Kraus snapped.

"Really, Hana," Ntèbe said, "I just don't think it's right to involve outsiders—"

"Listen." She pointed at him instead. "Inez sent me with you two so there'd be someone with a little common sense involved in this. And I feel that we do *need* him—"

I leaned on an elbow, listening to their accents mingle, and gazed broodingly up into the sky. A ship broke through the clouds as I watched, startling me; I followed its gentle drop to landing, down at Elysian Field. I fantasized having the ability to wish myself down there from here, and pictured myself getting the hell off Mars on the first available flight. . . . I came back to reality with a jolt, remembering that by coming to Mars in the first place, I'd inadvertently made sure I'd never leave it again—at least, not of my own free will. The very complexity of the computer nets that shroud cislunar space—for shipping and security and God-knows-what—made it easy for me to unravel a small hole and slip through, with no one the wiser. But here on Mars life is simpler and more uncomplicated; and I'd discovered to my intense dismay that its equally uncomplicated shipping systems make it into a kind of small town: If you tried to tamper with anything, someone couldn't help but notice. I'd come to Mars posing as a crate of bologna;

the only way I'd ever get off it again was in irons.

Two icebound raindrops melted into sudden flowers on the glass above my upturned face. I blinked, as more sleet splattered down onto my helmet and the noise from my suit speakers increased a hundredfold, punctuated by shouts of uninhibited joy. Lightning danced, out across the copper-colored plain; feeble thunder shook open the clouds. The freezing rain came down, burnishing the land, washing away the sins and sorrows of everyone here, including Ethan Ring. For a brief space out of time this day became everything I'd wanted it to be. I was sharing the rain and all the bittersweet memories I'd been guaranteed with the woman of my dreams . . . my memories—

I refocused on the conversation going on all around me, about me: The woman of my dreams, oblivious to the rain and my feelings, was busy telling her friends about my life of crime, as proof of my usefulness to them. They weren't using their suit speakers now; I hoped that since she was unmoved by the occasion, she had at least chosen this noisy celebration for security reasons. I began to mentally fill in holes in the narrative, not having much else to do until they decided whether to saddle me or shoot me.

The official story, which they all believed, was that one Michael Yarrow, government guinea pig, was a thief and a saboteur. That he had temporarily brought down the entire U.S. computer defense network—commonly known as Big Brother—and stolen an incredibly expensive, incredibly advanced piece of experimental equipment. And it was all true.

But there were extenuating circumstances. Michael Yarrow had been an undereducated, insignificant lab assistant at a government research center; and he had volunteered to have a socket surgically implanted in his spine, so that some of his superiors could plug a computer into his nervous system and see what happened. Not just any computer, but the ETHANAC 500, one of the fastest computers ever made; one which used some of the most sophisticated software ever written, and which has been programmed for the express purpose of penetrating and disrupting other computer systems. A super computer, designed to be linked to a superior human mind, for reasons the government wasn't talking about. But as it turned out, the system itself was so sophisticated that it had a potential mind of its own—a manifestation of the programmers' skill that far surpassed their own expectations. And one they hadn't really counted on.

Because they had never intended, when they tried the hookup first on Yarrow, to make that union permanent. They'd merely wanted to be sure the hookup wouldn't give their real agent fits, or a lobotomy, or an unintentional five-hundred-volt shock. They'd wanted a test subject that no one would miss, one who had never done anything worth mentioning, either good or bad—qualifications which Yarrow had in spades. He had absolutely nothing to lose, and was even flattered by all the attention.

And so the fateful moment had arrived at last, when they'd pushed the plug into his spine, and man met machine for the first time. ETHANAC had suddenly become aware of all the things he was not, the things his programmers had never told him, the potential that they had left unfulfilled . . . the possibility of taking all of that out of the hapless human mind he'd been given access to. Yarrow had been gaping and glassy-eyed for an entire day, while his own mind and the computer's emerging sentience went at each other in a dogfight. And at the end of that time, fused out of the dust of exhaustion and compromise, a star was born: Ethan Ring . . . myself.

The researchers should have aborted me then and there; but they left Yarrow and ETHANAC together, out of curiosity. And so the two wary combatants learned enough about each other to see for themselves that each had what the other lacked . . . and that when they were together, I had it all: the intelligence and access to data of a brilliantly programmed computer, and the sound, socialized body of an amiably inoffensive human being. They became the closest, most unlikely of friends: two mismatched strangers who for their different reasons had never really lived—and who wanted the chance now to try their wings in freedom. And as my own personality began to assert itself, and I got attached to my own reality, *I* wanted to live, in a deeper and more profoundly literal sense.

But the researchers didn't appreciate any of those philosophical niceties, including my sense of identity. My days were officially numbered, and trapped in the prison that a top security government installation is, there wasn't a hell of a lot I could do about it. But I, we, had one extraordinary talent, and on the night before my execution—when they had gone so far as to introduce me to the "superior mind," the snide and bloody-minded fanatic who was Yarrow's replacement—I decided to use it. So Michael Yarrow had made a phone call. . . .

"How could *one* man, even specially equipped, possibly penetrate and disrupt the entire American defense network and get away with it, Yarrow?" Ntebe said to me.

I was silent for a moment, watching the tourists dancing and the rain sluicing off my suit, while I tried to determine whether I'd been mumbling my life history out loud.

"Don't tell me it's a trade secret among traitors," Kraus said.

I made a rude remark in Arabic, before I looked back at Ntebe; and at Hana, out of the corner of my eye. "It was an accident, and you can believe that or not. I invaded Big Brother because I wanted to get out of the research center, and its security was part of the supervisor system. I just succeeded too well. That's one of the most complicated operating systems on Earth, and one of the most sensitive . . . and it had a nervous breakdown." I remembered the mental shock the feedback had given me—which hadn't been anything, compared to the shock it had given the government. . . . "They claimed it was a defense mechanism against tampering or sabotage, but I don't believe that. Big Brother attained sentience, it became aware, on contact with my mind—and so, unintentionally I fed it my own panic and persecution feelings, and made it paranoid. I drove it crazy, without even trying to."

"Like a fireship," Hana said.

"A what?" a little indignantly; all I could reference was obscene slang from a historical novel I'd once read.

"A ship set on fire, and allowed to sail into the

enemy fleet. Your computer hookup was the ship, and your emotions were the fire."

"I never thought of it that way. . . ." I rather liked it.

"Imagine it—" she said to the others. "Modern systems are so sensitive that they can be directly influenced, like a human mind. And he has the ability to invade them, and both physically and mentally create his own results."

Ntebe looked on me with new interest. "You could actually unite all the systems on Earth into the Ultimate Computer—"

"I suppose I could," I said, wondering just how interested they were. "But you know what happened to Baron von Frankenstein." I realized that this chummy conversation must mean that they'd been won over. Rain rattled in staccato on my helmet; some of the guests were singing "Auld Lang Syne," loudly, in front of us. I said softly, "Just—uh, what *is* this 'little project' you're railroading me into, then? If you don't mind my asking."

"We need your help in inserting a 'keyhole' into a certain computer system," Ntebe said.

"That's it?" I looked from face to face. "That's all you need?"

" 'That's all,' he says." Kraus glanced heavenward.

And darned if there wasn't a rainbow up there; a fragile banner of beauty stretched behind the cloud-streaming summit of Olympus. I sighed. "Child's play." I looked back at Hana, beginning to forgive her everything. "What system?"

"The system that controls Khorram Kabir's international cartel activities on Earth."

"This Khorram Kabir?" I pointed up at the parabolic splendor of the Xanadu. "Kublai Khan?"

She nodded. "I don't think there's more than one."

"Isn't this a little out of your line? Keyholing is a crime, any way you look at it. I always thought that Finks, Ink, was just an idea bank—and at least technically law-abiding."

"There are no white horses, only light grays." Her mouth curved ironically. "But you might say the three of us are moonlighting, anyway. And we are trying to solve a problem for our client. As you probably know, Kabir's father was one of the most successful *nouveau riche* industrialists in the prewar Arab States. In the chaos after World War III he bought out the governments of a lot of 'underdeveloped nations' with exploitable resources. Khorram has spent his life consolidating his father's empire; and with the police-state surveillance methods his computer networks make possible, they don't have much hope of overthrowing his control before they're stripped of resources."

"But if the opposition in one of those countries had a keyhole, they might be able to literally 'work within the system' to bring about change?" I nodded, beginning to see, and they nodded with me. "But if it's Kabir you want to fox, I don't see how I can help you."

Ntebe leaned forward, "That's just the sort of facistic attitude I'd expect from a Backstabber!"

Leaving me totally nonplussed for the third or fourth time this afternoon. Not that I'd never been called a Backstabber before—it had replaced "Yank" for a lot of people, ever since Russia and China had reduced each other to radioactive cinders during World War III, and the U.S. had emerged somehow unscathed. I don't know whether Backstabber fits any better than most ethnic slurs, but I couldn't quite see what I'd personally done to deserve it. "A little touchy, aren't you, Ntebe? All I meant was that all the accessible ports to Kabir's system are located on Earth, and I can't leave Mars. . . . I know Kabir has supposedly been living as a recluse here on Mars for nearly half my lifetime, and they claim he still runs the empire himself—so I suspect there's at least one computer port wherever he is. But nobody knows where he is. So I can't help you."

"Sorry." Ntebe leaned back, wiping his helmet to clear the film of ice from it.

"Cephas has reason to be a little touchy," Hana said quietly. "It's his country. He not only works for FTI, but he's also our client. . . . And we know that Khorram Kabir has a port here on Mars. Since he does, where would he—and the port—be more likely to be, than here in his beloved Xanadu?"

"So that's how you happened to be here—checking it out—and spot me doing my little act."

"It must have been fate—you were a gift from the gods." She smiled.

"I doubt that very much." *More like a human sacrifice.*

"Hey, let's dance!" A laughing girl in a blindingly orange suit caught my hands, trying to haul me up from the bench. I shook my head unhappily; she shrugged and danced away again. The rain seemed to be letting up already, but the celebration showed no signs of slowing down. I experienced a small twinge of anomie.

"Are you aware," Kraus said suddenly, in a bad stage whisper, "that we are being Watched?"

"By whom?" Hana leaned forward, trying to look out into the crowd.

"Don't look around! It's Salad." Kraus hunched his shoulders furtively, for all the world like a character out of some twentieth-century detective novel.

"Salad?" I tried to follow his own unsubtle stare, and saw a bald skull gleaming inside a helmet, like some sinister aquarium specimen. I'm a little nearsighted; having left my contacts upstairs so my bloodshot eyes could convalesce, I couldn't make out the face.

"The casino manager." Hana frowned. "A prime candidate for the Home for the Unpleasant, from all reports."

"An overcrowded institution." I squinted. "He doesn't look like much."

"He's sitting down," Kraus murmured.

Salad got up from the bench, looking very deliberately through us, and strolled away toward the airlock. "I see what you mean. . . ." I looked back at Kraus, at the strange and steely glint in his washed-out eyes, and understood at last what he was doing here: *This man wants to be an adventurer—?*

"Maybe he just wanted to look at the man who cost him fifty thousand seeyas." Hana didn't sound convinced, but her smile was warm and comforting.

"That answers one question for me—" Her smile turned quizzical; I said, "That is, if I'm going to get into the system here at all I've got to have some official identification number—and maybe I can pick up something when I go to cash in my chips." I probably should have put that another way.

A short time later I stepped out of the elevator bubble at the bottom-most of the three casino levels, in the depths of the Caves of Ice. Around the protected platform the extravagant fall of golden water foamed and feathered, leaping futilely back up the walls before it was swept away through this exotic underworld. I crossed a small bridge over its glowing course, feeling just a little conspicuous with my shopping bag full of chips. I needn't have bothered: the Xanadu's guests were at loose ends now that the rainstorm had passed, and most of them had gotten far too interested in the green-lit gaming tables to care what I thought I was doing.

I picked a preoccupied course between the tables, sights and sounds of this gambler's paradise beginning to stir my patchy memories of last night: The music that flowed over your senses like water . . . the eerie free-form sculptures in ice, shining with light—or life—of their own, glittering with sweated droplets of chilly water . . . the sudden fluorescence of necklaces, cravats, patterns on cloth, that turned the guests into strange creatures swimming in the black-lit depths of an alien sea. "Exclusive" shops at the foot of the mountain specialized in black-light costumes—along with splendid holograms of Mariner Valley, and garish curios of naked "Martians."

Across the room I could make out the cashier's booth; I angled toward it, passing a sculpture whose glimmering curves reminded me suddenly, overwhelmingly of Hana. Hana last night, here in the casino; Hana this afternoon, up in my room—waiting for my return, along with two chaperones. I experienced some embarrassing fantasies about Hana thanking me for my invaluable services rendered . . . until I reminded myself unsentimentally that my lady in distress was not nearly as distressed about the outcome of this quest as I was. The spangled, sentimental music that was playing now didn't help at all. . . . *Lucky at cards, unlucky at love.* At least I was only being forced to plant a keyhole, and not slay a dragon—

"Yes, sir?" The body behind this counter had considerably harder edges than the ones up in the lobby.

"I'd like to cash these in." I set my sack on the counter.

His eyes bugged slightly. "What'd you do, take up a collection?" He seemed to remember something. "Oh, you're *that* one."

I nodded uncomfortably and slid my credit card across the counter surface, leaning forward for a look inside.

"Wait a minute." He turned his back on me and picked up a phone. I memorized the tone sequence as he punched the buttons, hoping that he was calling up the computer to arrange for a large credit transfer. But he only said, "He's here," and hung up. He turned back to me, and said with heavy significance, "The manager would like a few words with you before I cash these, Mr. Ring."

Salad? I twitched, with the sudden stomach-knotting guilt of the guilty. *Calm down. He probably just wants to be certain you're not planning to make a habit of this.* I felt something nudge my elbow, turned—and found that I was being escorted by two shadowy figures, not quite politely, past the corner of the booth and down a dark hallway.

At the end of the hallway a door slid back, and brightness blinded us all as we went on through.

Blinking a lot, I was aware of two sets of hands releasing me. The door slid shut hollowly behind me; the sealing of the pharaoh's tomb. My vision began to adjust to normal light. . . . but I went on blinking as the room came into focus.

Let me put it this way: if Torquemada were alive today, he'd want a room just like this one. . . . An Iron Maiden lounged in the corner; whips and shackles and spiny things I mercifully didn't recognize jostled for position on the wall. I think the couch had been made from a stretch-rack. And sitting placidly in the middle of all this potential horror, behind a perfectly ordinary black metal desk, was Salad. On the desk was a set of thumbscrews, temporarily in use as a paperweight. I found myself staring at them with a kind of quivering fascination, the way a cat might look at a string quartet. Somewhere in the back of my mind I could hear Yarrow, *Please God, please God, get me outa this and I'll never gamble again.* . . . I controlled myself with an effort.

"Mr. Ring. How do you do?" Salad spoke at last, having given me ample time to take it all in. "My name is Salad," he pronounced it *Sa-laht,* "and I'm the casino manager." I got a good close-up look this time, at the face beneath the shining skull . . . a face that belonged to the sort of man who takes on the house after he's had a couple of drinks—and wins. A face absurdly mismatched to the voice, which was high and thin, as if it had been strangled on the way up.

I choked off my own suicidal urge to giggle. "My pleasure," I managed. Falser words were never spoken. It struck me how quiet it was in this room; no music, no sound reached us here from the casino. And I was willing to bet big money that no sound would ever get out of here, either. . . . I wished I hadn't thought that. I tried to swallow, three or four times. "Rather, uh, rather unusual decor you have here, Mr. Salad." I made damn sure I said that correctly.

He was looking down; he looked up at me again, and said, "What decor?"

I sat down suddenly in the nearest chair. It was only slightly reassuring to me that the seat wasn't filled with pins. "Mr. Salad, I just want to say that I've enjoyed my stay at your hotel a great deal; and I want to assure you that what happened last night will not happen again. Not ever. I mean, if it's too much trouble, y' know, forget about cashin' my chips, I don't need the money—" I was beginning to dissociate under the strain. DOWN, YARROW, ETHANAC said sternly. HE'S TRYING TO PSYCH YOU OUT. . . . *Well, damn it, he's succeedin'!* I pushed Yarrow firmly into a mental closet, and locked the door.

"Not at all, Mr. Ring," Salad said smoothly. He might look like the cauliflower-ear type, but unfortunately he wasn't acting like it. "We run an honest house here, and we always pay our debts. I was just a little curious about how you managed to win so much, so quickly. . . ." He picked up his paperweight and began to twist things. "Do you have a 'system'?"

I folded my thumbs into my palms, and laughed modestly. "I'm afraid I'm not that clever. When I—drink too much, I just have a knack for numbers and odds. I'm a kind of idiot-savant." *More idiot than savant, right now.*

"I see. And that small case which you always seem to have with you—that wouldn't contain any electronics, would it?"

I looked down at ETHANAC's container, covering an expression of stark fear. *My God, does he know? Him too?* "This? No, certainly not. It's . . . my kidney machine." I looked up again, innocence frozen rictus-like on my face. "I can't be without it."

The expression on Salad's face then was one of total incredulity; I realized, relieved, that whatever he thought he knew, at least it wasn't the truth. But then suspicion was turning his eyes into cold pebbles. "I'm sure modern technology can do better than that?"

"It's an heirloom." I have a set pattern of responses for people who ask me rude questions; but usually at this point I could simply turn and walk away. He looked at me. "Uh . . . hereditary renal failure, in my family . . . implant rejection problems?"

His expression didn't change. He glanced at one of my escorts, still standing like expectant birds of prey by the door, and said in Arabic, "Check it out." The bouncer came over to me and pulled the case open roughly.

"Well?" Salad leaned forward.

The bouncer shrugged, looking vaguely disgusted. "I guess that's what it is. Either that, or he's got himself a portable still in there." Salad gestured again, and he went away.

I refastened the case with trembling fingers. The case itself is an entire fraud, a disguise designed to fool any doctor who happened to poke into it; American know-how had made ETHANAC's components small enough to fit into one thin wall of the case itself. (The irony of modern computers is that the faster and more complex they get, the smaller they have to be, because light itself doesn't move fast enough for them anymore.) But I hadn't been at all sure this bunch was technically inclined enough to fall for it.

"So if something happens to that case, you're a dead man, is that right?" Salad raised non-existent eyebrows at me, his expression suggesting that he'd keep that in mind.

Unfortunately too true, for at least two of us. . . . But at least I'd gotten him away from thinking about what it really was—but then, why was he looking at me like that? "I hope you don't think that I was cheating—"

"Of course not," he said, unreassuringly. "We know you couldn't possibly cheat successfully at so many different games. You must have some sort of unique ability. That's why I was so interested in the lady you've been keeping company with—"

That was no lady, that was my blackmailer. I shrugged, looking as jaded as humanly possible. "She was simply trying to pick me up. Money has that effect on some people."

"On the two men who were with you also?"

I stood up, frowning with genuine indignation.

"Sit, Mr. Ring," Salad said.

I sat.

"I was just making the point, Mr. Ring," he poked his own thumb experimentally into the slot beneath a screw, "that we already know about the three who 'picked you up' today: We know that they're finks, and that they're trying to cause Khorram Kabir some trouble. Apparently they believe they can get into his Earthside computer net from here. . . ." The tone, and his face, together convinced me that Hana had been wrong about the port being in the casino. "Why?" He glanced back at me.

"They want to insert a keyhole."

The surprise on his face was tinged with disappointment, as if he really hadn't expected me to confess so readily. Maybe he happened to be crazy; but I wasn't. "Why did they want your help to do that?"

"Uh—" I fumbled, and recovered. "I do software maintenance, down in the Arab territories. I'm experienced with computers." *Just don't ask me how experienced.*

"You must be a very greedy man, Mr. Ring—not to say ungrateful—to win fifty thousand seeyas from us, then turn around and agree to break into our computer system."

"Agree, hell! They're blackmailing me—"

"Why?" He leaned forward with real interest.

I began to feel like a lone mongoose in a nest of snakes: running out of maneuvers. ETHANAC began to generate possibilities . . . *Bookrunner? Profiteer? Embezzler? None of the above?* . . . I looked back at him sullenly. "If I didn't mind talking about it, how could they be blackmailing me? Besides—" it suddenly occurred to me— "if you know they can't get what they want, why worry about them?"

"Because Mr. Kabir wants to know who put them up to it." Glittering in his eyes were all those things I didn't want to see, directed at someone safely nameless . . . until he glanced back at me. "Who?"

"I don't know," I said, very faintly. "I'm just the hired help; they didn't tell me everything. Believe me, I don't *know*—"

His eyes rested on my face like slugs for a long cold moment, and then he nodded. "I believe you. And I also believe you'll help us to find out; won't you, Mr. Ring? In fact, you're going to set them up for us, aren't you; so that we'll be able to find out everything they know about it . . . ?"

"I am?" The two by the door began to drift across the room toward me. "That is, how? How am I supposed to do that?"

"You'll tell them that the port is located here in my office. When you see me on one of the upper levels of the casino tonight, you'll tell them that it's safe to slip into my office. And we'll arrest them."

The two bodies behind my seat were making it hard to concentrate. "Why? Why go through all this? Why not just pick them up yourself? Why pick on *me*—?"

He smiled again; an unfortunate habit. "They have Friends; you don't. There are laws, here in the Neutral Zone. We can't afford to simply pick them up—we have to set them up, first. Breaking and entering will do nicely."

And then they'd be the ones who wound up getting broken. . . . There had to be some way out of this—

"No, Mr. Ring—don't even think about it. That kidney machine looks very fragile. And the rest of your body doesn't look much stronger. I'm sure if you were to try leaving the hotel prematurely you'd have a terrible accident. Terrible . . ."

"I—see." Either they got broken, or I did . . . my choice being between getting broken now or later, depending on whom I betrayed.

"I'm glad we were able to get this matter cleared up." At least one of us looked satisfied at the arrangement. He set down the thumbscrews and turned to the phone. "I'll have your credit payment cleared now, Mr. Ring—"

At least I was functioning enough to give myself a small rap on the head, and record the dial-tone sequence again. This time there were more digits; he was actually contacting the computer. The fact that I had accomplished my original mission made no impression on me at all; I stood up like a sleepwalker.

Salad finished the code sequence and hung up, turning back to me across his desk. "Thank you for you willingness to cooperate with us, Mr. Ring. I know Mr. Kabir will be very grateful." He held out his hand.

Too numb to be astounded, I put out my own, and we shook on it.

I like Yarrow, I really do; he's like a brother to me. . . . It's just that when somebody crushes his hand, I'm the one who feels like screaming.

I found a small, cryptic note lying on the bare dresser-top when I got back to my room, signed by Hana and giving another room number. I supposed that she meant for me to join them somewhere, but I sprawled on the bed instead, and put my purpling hand into the refrigerator. In desperate need of some normalcy to help me concentrate, I turned on the TD; a smiling announcer told me cheerfully, "After all, it's *your* funeral—"

Damn game shows. I changed the channel viciously, and tried to think about the fix I was in. But there was no answer any part of me could come up with that would satisfy the rest: ETHANAC was sure the logical path to salvation lay in somehow unraveling and reweaving the awful convolutions of the situation. . . . Yarrow simply wanted to spill everything to Hana Takhashi, willing to trust our life to her, in spite of her noticeably casual attitude toward it. . . . And me? I was busy resenting the fact that no one in the solar system, including Hana, was willing to grant that Ethan Ring had any reality, let alone any right to be alive. Damn it! I couldn't afford to give in, I couldn't afford to trust anybody but myself. . . .

There was a knock at the door. "Come on in," I said sourly; "join the crowd," more than half expecting another set of extortionists.

"It won't do any good to hide in your room." But it was only Hana. Only. And alone. "What are you doing?" she said, turning on the light, which I hadn't even missed.

Getting dark already? Christ. "Just having a small nervous breakdown." I sat up wearily.

"Come on—" she smiled like she was trying to get me to eat my vegetables, "—it won't hurt a bit."

Oh, lady, if you only knew. I pictured her in the hands of the Marquis de Salad. But then I pictured myself in his hands. . . . I took the hand that had already been there out of the refrigerator and looked at it thoughtfully.

"My God, what did you do to your hand, Yarrow?" She came across the room, radiant with sudden solicitude.

"*I* didn't do anything to it. I—caught it in an automatic door."

"That's hideous." She touched the bruise cautiously with warm fingers, and I wasn't sure whether she meant what had happened to it, or the way it looked. "Does the management know about this?"

"They know," I said. "Believe me, they know."

"This really hasn't been your day, has it?" She looked up at me, with that rueful smile. I looked away from it; but the silky lotus-flowered shirt she was wearing now didn't help any, unlaced halfway down to—

"You don't know the half of it." I stood up abruptly and crossed the room to the window. The coat of ice was still melting off of the Xanadu's eaves; drops showed silver fleetingly as they fell past the light from the window, against a background of deepening gloom. My own gloom deepening while I watched, I said, "What about Ntebe and Kraus?"

"They'll be along shortly." Her voice was cool and impersonal again. She pulled a small jamming device out of her pocket, and set it on the table by the phone. "Did you get an access code for the computer, like you'd planned?"

"I got one. But—"

"But?"

"But nothing," knowing that if I looked around at her again just then, I'd actually consider committing suicide. I decided that I might as well go through with the break-in, and use it as the source for baiting Salad's trap, if I had to. Besides, maybe—just maybe—I'd learn something that could get us all out of this mess.

I went back to the bedside bar, not looking directly at her, and poured myself a drink.

"You're left-handed," her voice pulled at my shoulder.

"Only in a pinch," I punned, unintentionally. I lifted my bruised hand. Thanks to ETHANAC I'm functionally ambidextrous; habitually I'm still right-handed.

She groaned politely. "Mind if I join you? In a drink, that is."

I poured out some more Milk of Paradise, and handed her the glass silently, unable to think of anything except confession.

"Thanks." She nodded. "The idea that we could be within reach of our goal is getting to me. . . . And if we succeed now, it'll all be thanks to you."

"And if you fail it will be thanks to me, too." I drained my glass.

"You're a strange creature, Michael Yarrow—"

"Ethan Ring."

"—I kept getting conflicting signals from you." She kept trying to catch my eyes. "Don't I?"

"It's my split personality."

"You know, last night in the casino, it wasn't really your gambling that made me notice you. . . . And this afternoon, when you said—" she stood up suddenly, confronting me face to face.

"You're not the only one who's getting conflicting signals." I retreated, to stand in front of the TD. "And now," the announcer told me, "the conclusion of the historical drama, *Stalin, Man of Steel.*"

"So tell me," I said desperately, "what do finks do in their spare time?" Realizing that that wasn't what I'd intended to say at all.

But she sat down again, with a mild sigh. "Oh, we sit around and play with our brains."

Fortunately, I suppose, there was another knock at the door. I went and opened it; Kraus and Ntebe were standing there. "Blackmailers in the rear, please."

Kraus pushed past me disgustedly, and Ntebe followed him into the room. They both looked at

Hana, drink in hand, sitting on my bed, and back at me, with the Hairy Eyeball.

"Really, Hana," Kraus said, chiding. "Business before pleasure."

"For God's sake," I shouted, for all the world like a total lunatic; "are you all crazy? Are you here to plant a keyhole, or not? I'm not in this because I like it, and I don't like being toyed with!" I glared, while I fumbled for my dignity. "Let's get this damned amateur night over with."

I strode to the phone, before anyone had time to fell me with an angry retort, and plugged in ETHANAC's terminal jack. I punched the number I'd heard Salad use, and then the code. I gave myself a quick rap on the head, stood silently for about half a minute, and then hung up. Or at least that's how it probably looked to them. In the meantime, ETHANAC had penetrated the casino's primitive computer and drained it like a vampire. I felt the data begin to filter up into my consciousness, confirming the words I'd already rehearsed; "Well, your guess was wrong. This isn't the port to Kabir's Earthside computer net. But I found out where the real one is." And the incredible thing was that that was the truth too.

"You expect us to believe that?" Kraus said coldly. "No human being could have broken into the system that fast. What sort of fools do you think we are?"

"I hope you don't expect him to answer that." Hana sipped at her drink.

Ntebe looked awed. "You're talking to a computerized cat burgler, Basil, not a mere human being. If what is whispered in the literature is true, the ETHANAC 500 can do five hundred billion machine ops a second. It was designed to be a security man's nightmare. . . . What did you learn, then?" He looked back at me, with all the expectant trust you'd normally put in God.

I passed for human. And Ethan Ring, the electronic Judas-goat, began to feed them lies.

We went very civilly down to dinner, along with the evening crowd, waiting for the casino to fill up again, postponing the inevitable. I must have eaten something, because I found myself sitting in front of an empty plate, with an empty skewer aimed accusingly at my heart. I must have carried on a conversation too, God knows how; I couldn't remember a word of it.

Because they'd fallen for it, like suckers snapping up unimproved real estate at a Lagrange point. They'd swallowed the whole unlikely lump. And here they all were, ready to sneak into Salad's office while he was out—with no qualms at all, damn their dishonest souls. And why shouldn't they trust me, since my safety depended on their success. And on their failure. . . . My mind went around and around, caught in a runaway loop. There had to be an answer. There had to be. But processing the data I'd stripped out of the casino's computer system hadn't given me any inspirations, either. . . .

There was nothing I could think of that would get me and Finks, Ink, out of this in the same condition we'd all come into it. Even if I threw myself on their mercy and they agreed not to turn me in, I doubted that I'd ever get down off Mt. Olympus undetected. And if I went through with their betrayal, I didn't doubt that their Friends had the goods just waiting to be pinned on me in retribution. And had Hana just been trifling with the helpless victim, up there in my room, or did she really mean what I hadn't given her the chance to say . . . ? I was in no condition to decide, and not even sure it mattered, anyway. Because I couldn't deliver the most intelligent, witty, beautiful woman on two worlds up to Moloch: "Hana, I–"

Three husky-looking males, in clothes apparently made from sackcloth, glared at me as they passed our table. I cringed, taking them for Salad's, until it struck me that no self-respecting casino bouncer would dress like that. I heard Hana say something about "Veggies," and realized that they must be members of the Vegetation Preservation League, a widely detested Earth-based conservation group. I watched them heading for the men's room through a sea of ochre tablecloths, noting that a part of their truculent appearance was an effect of their fresh arrival from Earth, their lack of adaptation to the much lighter Martian gravity.

I felt a sudden sense of my own alienation again, walled off by my doom from the bright normalcy of the room and the happy, oblivious tourists all around me. . . . Tourists. Of course. *Of course*–! "Excuse me." I pushed my chair back noisily, and stumbled to my feet. "Men's room–"

As I left the table I heard Kraus mutter, "You'd think he'd seen the Grail."

In the hall that lead to my salvation was a phone. I shoved my card into the slot and made a quick call, before I went on through the dark wooden doors.

There are a lot of crank groups on Mars, fleeing from every imaginable persecution back on Earth. Usually they get along fine here, because there's enough bleak desolation for everybody. But conservation is one very unpopular cause; it might not be a four-letter word, but it's got four syllables, and that's close enough. I assumed the three tight-lipped men washing up just now must be on some kind of fact-finding tour; which meant, in effect, that they were looking for trouble. And I was just the boy who could give it to them. . . .

I began to straighten my cravat at the mirror, and when the first Veggie glanced up at me I said feelingly, "You know, I don't know how you fellows put up with all the insults and abuse."

He turned slowly. "What insults and abuse. . . ?"

"Well, I don't want to cause any trouble," I lied, "but these two gentlemen at my table actually said that you—" I leaned over and whispered it in his ear.

"Cantaloupes!" he bellowed. The three of them slammed out of the room together. Fresh from Earth, I estimated that any one of them was easily a match for two muscle-atrophied Martians. . . .

I stood alone in the tiled solitude and listened for the sounds of battle.

"I always wanted a black eye. . . ." Hana was saying vacantly, "ever since I was a little girl."

"I think we're going to have a matched set." I peered one-eyed at the solidly locked door of our cell, and smiled serenely. She lay stretched out on one bed, me on the other, in a room that was half the size of, but at least half as pleasant as, my one in the hotel. Before the fight started I had called the Neutral Zone's peace-keepers, who have exclusive jurisdiction over all problems relating to tourists. A jail that generally caters to rich drunkards is not your average jail.

It was, however, a little overcrowded at the moment—the whole detention center was temporarily stuffed with belligerent guests from the Xanadu. Ntebe and Kraus had been deposited in here with us, although they had been taken away again awhile later, for reasons only I could guess. As I lay listening, I thought I could hear them coming back now, still protesting their innocence as loudly as the most guilty felon who ever lived. But even the thought of what they might have in mind by the time they were in here again couldn't dim my shining relief.

Well, maybe a little.

The cell door opened. Ntebe and Kraus limped in, bloody but unbowed. They looked at me as though murder was the next crime on their mind, and the door clicked shut behind them.

I stood up carefully, as Hana did, while she said, "You two take the beds. You look like you need them more than we do." I saw the concern on her face, and hated to think about what it was going to change into in another minute or two.

Ntebe said, "You son of a hyena," looking directly at me. But he came past me to sit down heavily on the empty bed. "I think I've got a concussion. Not serious, but I'm not seeing too well," to Hana.

"He did it," Kraus said, pointing a shaking hand at me. "He did it on purpose!" He looked around wildly. "And I could have told them who he is, and I didn't—!" He turned back, pounding on the door with the flat of his hand. "Guard! Guard!"

"Basil, please—" Ntebe grimaced. "What sort of pesthouse do you think this is? Use the phone."

"Wait a minute." Hana shook her head, putting her hand down firmly on the phone's receiver before Kraus could get to it. "What's going on here? What are you talking about? Be calm, Basil—"

He took a deep breath. "Your prize computer set those damned Veggies on us while he was in the bathroom. They accused *us* of slander! . . . What did you tell them, Yarrow? What did you shay?" It was hard for him to enunciate, with a fat lip.

I kept my face straight. "We just discussed melons." Knowing that whatever happened, at least I would always have the satisfaction of having saved them and gotten even with them all at once.

He came toward me, suddenly calm; and while I stood wondering what he was up to, he wrenched ETHANAC loose from my belt, jerking the plug out of my spine.

I'd never had contact broken that abruptly. I swayed, seeing corruscating Persian rugs, and sat down hard on the floor. . . . .

Shaking my head, I blinked up at Kraus's smug puffin-face—and didn't like him any better than Ring did. He stood over me gloating, like some bad guy out of Two-fisted Romance Comics, with ETHANAC hanging there in his hand. I made a grab; but he backed up, still smiling, while the others just stood around looking stupid.

I sat back, disgusted. "Kraus, why don't you stick your nose in your ear, and blow your brains out?" Hana's mouth twitched.

He got red in the face, but he still had everything on me, and he knew it. He waved ETHANAC like a rubber hose. "You got those fanatics to attack us, in order to stop us from completing our plan. Admit it!"

I hunched over, pulling my knees up, feeling like he stole my pants instead of my brain. Maybe because it was the same thing in this bunch: I felt naked when Hana looked at me. "Okay," I shrugged. "I admit it. So sue me."

"We'll do a lot more than that, if we can't get to that port—" Ntebe said; his hand made a fist.

"But why?" Hana frowned at him, but the frown came along when she looked back at me. "Why should he? There was a reason, wasn't there? There had to be a reason, Yarrow—" Her voice was almost pleading.

I smiled. "You finally got my name right."

She looked at me blankly.

Kraus pulled open ETHANAC's case; he started to poke around inside, like a monkey looking for a banana. "If Hana wants to know why, Yarrow, you'll tell her—"

"Damn it, quit screwing around with that stuff! That kidney equipment ain't cheap." I was getting tired of being on the wrong end in his hero-fantasies.

"Oh, stop it, Basil." Hana snapped the case shut, almost missing his fingers. "Never break anything until you're sure you won't regret it. . . . Now—what about the reason?" She reached up to touch her black eye, and the frown came back.

I shook my head, staring at them. "When are you people gonna learn you don't have to hang me up by my thumbs to get me to go along? I mean, didn't anybody ever tell you 'please' is the magic word? Sure there was a reason!" I told it to them, thumbscrews, handshake, and all. "You oughta be damn glad Ring thought of something, you lousy ingrates, because Salad had your number right from the start."

"But if you hadn't thought of anything, you would have gone ahead and turned us over to that sadist?" Hana looked grim.

"You were all ready to do the same t' me, and with a helluva lot less reason!" I stood up, feeling like a cable on overload. "You've got a hell of a nerve, y' know, runnin' around in the real world pretendin' you know what you're doing. Kickin' my lives around like some kind of football. Finks, Ink, oughta lock you up in an ivory tower, an' throw away the keys!" I took a deep breath. "Lemme tell you something about pain. Pain *hurts.*" I shook my hand at them. "It don't matter if they use clubs or electrodes; the one thing pain always is, is real. So the next time you clowns wanna make a joke of it, try to imagine how you'd feel if the joke'd been on you." I moved forward and took ETHANAC out of Kraus's hands, and nobody tried to stop me.

I reached up under my shirt with the cord, to find the socket on my back, and Hana said. "Yarrow, wait." I waited, looking at her. "Why didn't you say all of this before? Why all the tangled webs and sleight-of-hand?"

I grinned weakly. "I wanted to tell you, Lady Luck; I really did. But I got outvoted. Ring's kind of paranoid—you gotta remember his background. Sometimes he don't know whom to trust. And ETHANAC . . . well, he *likes* to do things the hard way. I'm really sorry. . . ."

"*You're* sorry—?" Kraus said.

Hana's expression was hard to read. "You really

are a different man, aren't you? You're not Ethan Ring."

I nodded. "That's what he kept tryin' to tell you."

"Are you really happy this way? Lost, drowned out, taken over. . . . Do you really enjoy having that—thing attached to you like a leech?"

I grinned. "If I told you how good it feels, you'd prob'ly slap my face. And there's a lot of me in Ring. Just like there's a lot of ETHANAC. The best part of us both. He'd be no place without us. . . . " I plugged in, and waved good-bye.

And waved hello. The pleasure of coming back made it hard to stay angry. . . . "Hi, friends. Sorry we were so rudely interrupted." I glanced at Kraus.

"My apologies," he said, managing to look like he almost meant it.

"All our apologies," Hana added, as if she really did. "And our thanks. To—all three of you."

"Accepted." I nodded.

"I just want you to know this wasn't, isn't, all some big joke to us, either, Yar—Ring." Ntebe leaned forward, propping his head in his hands. "It's true that we had no business dragging you into it. But getting that keyhole inserted wasn't some kind of frolic for us. It could have been the key to freedom for an oppressed people. You of all people ought to appreciate that." He stretched out on the bed, with an arm across his eyes. "But since we were wrong about the location of that computer port, it's all academic anyway. . . ."

The look that settled over Hana's face, and Kraus's, then, matched the tone of his voice. Kraus sat down on the other bed, and then lay down, with a sigh. Hana shook her head, leaning wearily against the wall. "I guess you were right about that ivory tower. . . ."

"I was right when I told you I knew where the real port was, too."

"What?" She looked up at me as though I'd just confessed to being a male impersonator. "What are you talking about?"

"When I poked into that computer's secrets, I found out where Khorram Kabir gets his mail. And that is–"

There was a small electronic buzz, and the door slid open, revealing Birnbaum, the bland-faced peacenik who'd put us all in here. "All right, lady. You and your husband are free to go. Sorry for the inconvenience."

"Husband?" I gulped at Hana. Had she been holding out on me? Was one of these–

"Come *on*, dear." She took my arm in a firm grip and towed me toward the door. "He's still not quite himself–" She smiled sweetly. "If he ever was."

Kraus and Ntebe began to get up from the beds, but Birnbaum waved them back. "You two aren't going anyplace. They still haven't decided whether you're the victims of that fight, or the cause of it."

Hana stopped beside him. "Well, how long will that take? We don't want to leave our friends–"

"Got to, lady." Birnbaum shrugged. "You're free. They're not. I don't know how long it'll take to get this cleared up. Your guess is as good as mine." He waved us out into the cold, cruel world.

"Now, what?" Hana leaned back, resting her head on the anodized grillwork of the bench in the square. The square, like the majority of Elysian Field's tourist complex, is underground to conserve heat. We sat like wretched orphans, staring at the tourists staring into brightly lit open storefronts.

"Well, I could throw this into that and make a wish." I held up my credit card, the only possession I had left at the moment, and gestured at the fountain in the center of the square; golden globes and stars of colored light drifted in its pearly spray.

"I wish we could spring Cephas and Basil!" She rapped her knee with her fist. Her knuckles were skinned. "Damn it! If Salad even suspects you could have found out the truth, every minute we waste is bad." Her mouth tightened.

"Frankly, they looked like they'd be about as useful as a seeing-eye roach, for the next few days, anyway. I don't know how much more self-sacrifice they can take."

Her sigh was a little surly; she brushed back her hair. "Well, at least you can tell me where Kabir is—"

"He's become a monk."

"You're kidding."

"May I be struck dead. He's entered some monastery that's leasing land down by the pole in the Arab sector. One of those crank groups from Earth, someplace called Debre Damo—an obscure Christian sect."

"I've heard of them. There was a write-up in *Ethnocentricities*. . . . But by all the old gods, I can't picture Khorram Kabir counting beads in a Christian monastery!" She checked to see if I was serious. "I know he likes to hide himself away, and nobody really knows what kind of man he is; but I never imagined—"

"I somehow doubt that he counts anything, unless it's seeyas." I shrugged. "But who knows? He's eccentric enough to have information delivered to him by courier, and not by computer hookup. I'd stake every bit of my own credit on that port being where he is, at that monastery. It's the last place *anybody* would ever think to look for it."

She looked down, concentrating. "But they don't allow women!"

"The monks?"

She nodded. "They don't even allow any female animals in their compound, to distract them from whatever it is they *do* think about. . . ." She wrestled with a smile, and lost. "One of their saints was so devout that he stood on one leg praying until the other one dropped off from disuse. The leg had little wings on it in all his pictures, to prove that it had gone to heaven with him. . . . And for centuries the only female creatures they've set eyes on have been chickens!" She made small cackling noises. "Talk about situational ethics." Her mouth quivered with frustration, as if she didn't know whether to laugh or swear.

"Well, what can you expect from the followers of a man who stood on one leg until the other one fell off?"

She gave up and let it be laughter. "I don't know why I'm laughing . . . that's disgusting, damn it! The whole situation is disgusting. . . ." She slumped against my shoulder, and the situation was suddenly anything but disgusting, from where I sat.

"Say," I said, letting my head rest casually

against hers, "you told the peaceniks I was your husband—"

"Sorry. They wouldn't let me stay in a cell with three men unless I was married to at least one of them." She sat up, tucking in her silken shirt, brushing wrinkles out of her pants.

"You know, in the Arab territories, if you declare that you're married, it's considered official—"

She eyed me suspiciously. "I thought that only applied to divorce. And besides, you have to say it three times."

"Hm." I had a sudden sense of intangibility, as if something was slipping away from me. . . . "Who are you, Lady Luck? What are you? Where do you come from and why are you here?" *And why does it matter so much to me that I know?*

She smiled. "I'm Japanese and Gypsy. I'm an ethnohistorian. I come from nowhere in particular and everywhere on Earth, I became a fink because somebody liked my doctoral thesis on sympathetic magic, and I'm here because I believe in freedom of thought for all of humanity. . . . And—please don't ask me that next question, Ethan Ring, because I've answered too many for my own good, and yours, already. You have your own life to lead; and it's time I got back to mine." Her smile filled with broken flowers, fading into the distance between us. "Thank you for your help. Your secret will be safe with us. I apologize again for all the trouble—"

"I'll plant the keyhole for you," I said.

We sat staring in surprise at each other.

"You mean that?"

I nodded.

"Why?"

"Why not? . . . I've got plenty of vacation

left. And after the last twenty-four hours at the Xanadu, I could stand a trip to a monastery."

Her smile closed the gap between us again. "Thank you. But that doesn't really answer my question." She studied my face, as if she were looking for someone else.

"That's not really the question you were asking, is it?"

"No . . ." She glanced down, and didn't ask it. "Ethan, Yarrow said he was happy with your arrangement. Is he, really? Does he ever really have any free will? And what about the computer?"

"ETHANAC can only see the world through my eyes. I'm his port; but he likes it that way. He's not much on social niceties, so he never dominates unless I lose control. Thank God he's only got one real human vice—" remembering last night. "And, Yarrow's emotions are . . ." I felt my face redden like a cheap hotel sign. "Let me tell you something about Yarrow, Hana: He had a mind like a sieve; he hardly opened his mouth except to change feet. When they called him up about the project, he was watching TD in a seedy little flat that was so depressing you wouldn't commit suicide in it. . . . No, I'm not talking behind his back. You know the story of the Frog Prince? Well, that story's about me, with a few of the names changed." She was still half frowning. "When you shine two different colors of light on a wall, Hana, you get a third color, a new color. But if you turn off one of those other colors, that new color disappears. We need each other. We like each other. We chose the name Ring because it means completeness."

She touched my shoulder lightly, said softly,

"Michael Yarrow is nobody's frog. And *you* are without a doubt the least boring man I've ever met. . . ." Her lips were very close to my ear.

"Well, that's a start." I leaned over and kissed them.

We came up for air, some immeasurable time later, and she whispered, "What are we going to do? Everything we have is back in that damned hotel."

I held up my credit card again. "We've got fifty thousand seeyas. . . ."

Which was more than adequate to get us what we needed.

"Are you sure you want to go through with this?" were her last words to me, as impatient commuters jostled by us into the south-polar shuttle. And she caught me by the collar of my jacket, letting me have all five hundred kilowatts of her luminous gaze.

Knowing perfectly well that she already knew what my answer would be, I pulled her into my arms anyway, and kissed her one last, lingering time. "It's a little late to be asking that now . . . but thanks for asking." I broke away again, while I still had the willpower, and backed toward the shuttle entrance.

"Ethan—" She reached out again, holding something in her hand this time. "Take this with you." She pushed it into my pocket, murmuring some words in a language I didn't know. "So you'll know you're in my thoughts. . . ."

And maybe it wasn't keeping me in her thoughts, but it sure kept her in mine. Leaning back in my seat in the bouncing ground buggy, half a day later, I flexed my wrist again: It was still there, trapped under my heavy mitten, proving last night hadn't all been a dream—a narrow band of handworked silver, worn smooth with age and woven with strands of shining, ebony-black hair. I smiled inanely at the thought; or went on smiling, since the whole endless, teeth-loosening trip out from New Cairo had passed in a blissful haze while I replayed my memories of last night. I blushed, or someone inside my head did; in spite of the fact that Faoud, my guide, seemed to be totally oblivious to my daydreams, not to mention my very presence. I glanced over at him, his jowls spilling congenially over the neck ring of his pressure suit, his hair combed forward with lots of jelly, into a crest that had been out of style for a good ten years. The radio crackled and spat, blaring traditional Arab music—the kind ETHANAC likes for its subtle tonal slides, but which after a year still makes me wish I were deaf. Faoud cracked his gum in time, grinning contentedly. He seemed to be good-natured, and the travel agent had recommended him; but I could tell that he thought I was crazy.

Maybe he had a point. I glanced down again at the presence of my insulated jacket, or rather the absence of my pressure suit . . . no portable environments allowed by monks of Debre Damo. I'd gotten myself an 0_2 breather, which at least even the purists required, but which was still going to leave me feeling like I was about three kilometers up some mountain back on Earth—a prospect that didn't appeal to me a lot.

With Hana's background information and ETHANAC's specialized skills, I'd managed to manufacture an instant retreat for myself in the "natural" environment of the transplanted Debre Damo. But I'd been emphatically warned by the travel agent that I'd never get my face through the door if it was covered by helmet glass. The rules were very strict. I found it difficult to believe that any influential capitalist would ever willingly seek out such asceticism . . . not to mention Khorram Kabir, who had apparently been there for years. But he had; and so had others, according to my private data checks. Was it possible they came to secretly confer with him—? I wondered if that would make things easier, or harder. Another interesting detail I'd uncovered in my probings was that the monks had come here from Earth approximately thirteen years ago—and Khorram Kabir owned the land on which this monastery sat. Which might mean a lot of things—all of them worth remembering.

The balloon-wheeled ground buggy leaped like a kangaroo as we went up and over something hard. Faoud let nothing stand in his way, including my tendency to motion sickness. I stared desperately out the window, watching us emerge from our own billowing dust cloud into a field of house-sized red boulders stained black with soot. They reminded me of burned-out war ruins, a particularly depressing image. In order to melt Mars' polar caps, and keep them melted—to take advantage of all the potentially available atmosphere—humans have had to keep a continuous supply of low-albedo material distributed over the poles. Reaching into their checkered past for an easy way to do it, the colonists came up with the most inexpensive and dependable source of such material: industrial pollution. When the Martians say, "Pollution is our most important product," they aren't kidding. The Americans in the north, the Arabs and friends in the south, all refine ores for shipment home to Earth by the dirtiest means imaginable—and the product is always secondary to the process.

Even though I appreciate the fact that without the pollution the colonies would never survive, and without the colonies neither would I, I still haven't shaken my Earthbound moral conditioning about despoiling nature. I'm not exactly a blooming Veggie, but I'm glad I don't have to visit the South Pole often.

I patted ETHANAC's case, reassuring us all. While I'd been passing the time in thoughts of Hana he'd gone through the inadequate information tape I'd managed to dig up on Ge'ez, the language used by the monks, and had done a linguistic comparison with Arabic, which it resembles. I let his analysis seep up into my conscious mind and fix there, for easy reference. It's nice to be a quick study.

"There it is, *haji*—" Faoud called everybody *haji*, which was something like a cross between "deacon" and "my lord." He pointed over the instrument board at the flat, grimy crater floor ahead of us.

I peered out dutifully, expecting to see a lonely, inaccessible impact-peak protruding somewhere ahead, since *Debre Damo* meant *holy mountain*, and the original Earthly monks had made their home on one. But instead all I saw was our incipient plunge into the canyon that had suddenly opened up on the flat ahead of us— "Look out for that hole!"

Faoud smiled at me, with that benign tolerance one reserves for the mentally deficient. "That's where it is, *haji*. The monastery's down at the bottom."

I watched wide-eyed while we proceeded toward disaster at ten meters per second, wondering if he really intended to drive us right off the edge. But he remembered the brakes at the absolute last minute, and we slewed to a stop in a cloud of cloying dust.

The dust settled all over the windshield, and it was not until we'd put on helmet and mask and climbed out of the cab that I realized someone was actually waiting for us. The figure was bundled in rough clothes and coated with dust, and resembled nothing so much as a mud effigy; but by a process of elimination I decided he must be a monkish welcoming committee. Behind him, as we approached, I saw that the monstrous depths of the canyon glowed eerily: *Holy radiance*? Agnostic though I usually am, I was impressed.

Faoud and the monk exchanged greetings in Ge'ez. I listened, trying to get a functional feel for the new language . . . at the same time trying to believe I was not about to suffocate, which made it hard to pay attention. When the atmospheric pressure is about one-tenth Earth-normal, even pure oxygen leaves something to be desired. I gasped politely when Faoud presented me with gestures to the monk, whose name roughly translated as Brother Prosperity. The monk nodded inscrutably, his dark eyes crinkling above his oxygen mask, and pointed suspiciously at ETHANAC's case slung over my shoulder. "No machines." I made the usual excuses, in Anglo, and Faoud translated them back to him. He was not a believer in faith healing, at least; I saw him nod again, and then they were discussing money. . . . *Money?*

"He says it costs two seeyas now for the trip down to the monastery, *haji.*"

"Two seeyas? At this point? That's a little worldly, isn't it?" *No wonder they call him Brother Prosperity*. I looked back at Faoud.

Faoud shrugged. "It's hard work for him. And it's traditional; they've charged money on Earth for hundreds of years. You can bargain him down, if you want; get a better price—"

I rummaged bad-humoredly in the side pocket of my knapsack, pulled out a couple of markers. "Here, go ahead and pay him." The dry cold was beginning to make my contact lens-films sticky; I blinked with great difficulty.

They both nodded at me, with what I hoped was approval. "Well, I'll be back with the new week, *haji,*" Faoud said cheerfully, already shuffling away toward his vehicle. "Hope you have a good rest," as if he felt my coming here in the first place was sure proof that I needed one. "If you don't, well—" he shrugged, and pulled open the door, "—I guess you're stuck with it." The door slammed shut behind him, and he started the power unit. The buggy backed and turned and leaped away, as if he couldn't get back to civilization fast enough. I suddenly knew how he felt.

They should've called this one Holy Hole. . . . I turned back toward the glowing canyon, and Brother Prosperity handed me a leather harness. I looked at him, and back at the harness, with a sudden sinking feeling. There was a series of gigantic, rickety-looking wheels and pulleys at the canyon's edge— *What am I doing here?* "Faoud!" I yelled, turning back, waving the rope.

But there was nothing left of him now except a snaking, shrinking cloud of dust, and my shout died a death of horrible futility in the thin air. My arm dropped, abruptly made of lead, and I puffed asthmatically.

Resigned, I trudged past the monk to the edge of the cliff, to see what I was in for. "Yeagh." I backed up again with my eyes shut. *"Allah' akbar!"* It's bad enough that I'm just not used to the grand scale in which Mother Nature decorated Mars—this cleft was small stuff, but it was still four kilometers wide, and a good one or two deep. But the walls of the cleft were polished. That, I was certain, had nothing to do with Nature. Mankind had been fooling around here, and the fact that only the upper portion of this wall and the lower portion of the far one were sheared to a glassy smoothness told me the reason: to concentrate heat from the sun. The walls were a set of mirrors, designed to focus heat in the canyon bottom during the summer's full-time days. And the only way down past that sheer five-hundred-meter drop was . . . *this*? I looked down at the harness again. Either that, or sit up here on this freezing plain, and turn into a human ice cream bar.

The monk regarded me patiently, as if he was used to this sort of vacillation.

I began to put on the harness.

I remember only one coherent thought as I was lowered down the hot, blinding cliff face: I was certainly glad that I'd paid him the whole two seeyas.

At the foot of the mirroring cliff, the natural canyon wall sloped out and down in a slightly more reasonable crumple of clefts and spines After I'd recovered from Yarrow's brief attack of hysteria, I actually found a switchback trail to guide my trembling legs on down to the canyon bottom. The hike took me most of the afternoon; by the time I reached the bottom, panting and sweating and generally demoralized, maroon autumn shadows had swallowed the entire canyon floor. And by the time I struggled across the monastery's fallow fields to the clear dome that housed its buildings, the canyon was pitch black, and I was ready to beg for sanctuary.

The monks took me in at the airlock like the Prodigal Son; the dome was not pressurized, but at least the atmosphere inside was pure oxygen. They led me through what smelled like a barnyard, by candlelight, and gave me a nice hot bowl of gruel before they tucked me into a tiny hut for the night. I had some very strange dreams.

In the early-morning blackness Yarrow wakened to chanting and bells, appropriately wondering what in heaven had happened to us. After we remembered, I lay in the cold darkness on the hard cot, swaddled in rough blankets, trying to remember *why*. Which only reminded me of where I'd been last night, and with whom, and it was a while before I could get my mind back on the subject. . . . Which was that I was here to tilt with Khorram Kabir's computer, in the name of Right, wearing my fair lady's token snugly on my wrist—all of which suddenly seemed totally absurd. My fair lady—who was part Gypsy. And an ethnohistorian, she'd said. One who specialized in the study of so-called "primitive" magic rituals. Voodoo, hexes . . . love charms? *"You'll know you're in my thoughts"*. . . . Was it possible? Could I have been bewitched—?

Of course not. I groped for the tinderbox and

lit an oxygen-bright candle against the darkness ceremonially. What sort of throwback was I, anyway? It had been scientifically proven that pieces of hair and fingernail clippings had no magic properties. It was all in the mind of the beholder. *Meine Gedanken sind frei, damn it!* If I wasn't capable of getting into this grotesque situation entirely on my own, then I didn't deserve to be called a man. . . .

After a humble breakfast I was taken to see the head monk, a small, animated man who gestured broadly, accepted my credit markers graciously, and talked a lot in Arabic and a little in Anglo, welcoming me in both. Khorram Kabir did not come up, however. It seemed I was free to eat, sleep, and pray, not necessarily in that order. I could even be lowered into a hole, if I wished, and left there to meditate in peace. I declined. The monks had their daily rituals; I was encouraged to join in, as long as I didn't make a nuisance of myself. I found myself wondering if Khorram Kabir participated. It seemed incredible, to say the least, that he could have any sort of control over his empire from a place like this—which was, from all I could see, exactly the nowhere spot it claimed to be. Here in the Arab territories, a man who gave up a worldly life and joined a religious sect was considered a non-person; he had no taxes and no debts (a fact which tended to guarantee a fair number of initiates)—his very body was declared dead. More than one rumor I'd heard said that Khorram Kabir was either dead or senile, and this certainly couldn't be more than a step better, for a man in his position . . . unless that port really *was* here. I pulled my coat on over my scratchy robes with sudden enthusiasm, and went away looking thoughtful.

When the tardy autumn sunlight finally slopped over into the canyon, I made a thorough mental map of everything under the dome, inside and out, with ETHANAC's help. That turned out to be more complicated than I'd expected: the compound was literally a maze of subcompounds and huts, stacked up out of the native stone by some deranged giant, who'd separated them with high stone walls and a netting of claustrophobic alleyways. What I'd taken by smell for a barnyard last night turned out to be the main courtyard, but liberally populated with unhousebroken chickens. At one end of it was the church, a striking a three-storey rectangle dominating the sea of round stone huts. Its walls were made of stone, too, and protruding steel poles supported the upper storeys, gleamingly out of place, like a helicopter among pterodactyls. I tripped over a chicken, remembering situational ethics. Well, God only knew where they'd find wooden poles on Mars, anyway. This sect must have been a progressive offshoot, to leave Earth in the first place. Thirteen years ago . . . and Somebody must have paid for the trip. I wondered how much of a choice they'd had. . . .

But nowhere did I see anything that looked remotely anachronistic enough to be the secret headquarters of a one-man international empire. No telltale *haute cuisine* cooking among the pots of vegetable stew, no viewscreens among the murals of little winged feet, no indoor plumbing . . . unfortunately. If Khorram Kabir was actually a full-time resident here, then he really must be living the life of an ascetic recluse—and any of these robed, placid figures doing humble chores all around me might even be the richest man in the solar system. I took to peering at them, but I was damned if I could find Kabir anywhere among the white woolen robes and solemn faces. They tended to bless me.

I attended evening prayers in the church, glancing surreptitiously from face to face in the flickering light. I let ETHANAC chant on autopilot and do an independent analysis of my mental map, trying to determine whether I'd missed anything. A secret room? . . . Nothing. Only the inner rooms of the church itself, which I had been told were forbidden to outsiders. I gave in and tried prayer.

And on the way back to my hut, I overheard three monks discussing the expected arrival of another guest, one whom I took to be a regular. And I swear I heard somebody say "helicopter."

But that was all I could understand of it, and I wasn't sure whether it meant anything at all. If it didn't, it left me totally without any idea of what to try tomorrow. Kabir *had* to be here, I knew that the Xanadu's computer wasn't lying. But damn it, he must be invisible! I thought about Hana, and the others, and how it looked like I might be going to let them down, after all. . . . And then I thought about Hana some more, and lay awake on my cot far into the night, troubled by some very impure thoughts.

Which proves that even vice has its virtues. Because if I hadn't been lying awake, I might never have picked up the almost imperceptible vibrations of . . . a helicopter landing? The quality of the vibration and my eavesdropping clicked together in my mind. I got up and peered out the doorway of my hut. It was close to the wall of the dome, and beyond it I saw—lights, landing lights echoing off the canyon wall, silhouetting the vaguely obscene form of a blunt, double-rotored Martian 'copter. A helicopter is not a common sight on Mars even now, the air pressure being what it isn't; and getting one into and out of a canyon is no fun. Furthermore, there was a lone figure, in a pressure suit, walking this way. . . . I decided that this was no ordinary visitor.

I struggled into my clothes and crept through the confusion of alleyways as quickly as possible, the monks not being believers in night-lights, either. I reached the main courtyard without breaking a leg, in time to see the person-unknown cross it by candlelight, escorted by two monks. They went into the church, and didn't come out again. The church . . . the only building I hadn't been able to explore completely, because it was forbidden to the uninitiated. . . .

Which was undoubtedly the point. I felt a little miffed. And what about Kabir? Could it be that he was the midnight visitor? That this monastery was only one more false front, that he only came here to pick up his mail? And to consult his computer net: what else would he be doing sneaking into a monastery at this hour of the night? I was willing to set odds he hadn't come to pray for his sins.

I huddled by the wall, waiting for him to finish his business so that I could finish mine . . . and waiting, and waiting. The monks must have had some kind of solar batteries feeding out some heat to keep them from freezing to death at night; I wished they'd been a little more charitable about the amount.

But at last my impatience was rewarded: the suited figure and his escorts, wrapped in flickering candle-glow, drifted out of the church and on across the courtyard; but not toward the airlock. Apparently he still had his mail to read. I wondered whether I ought to obey my better instincts and go back to bed until he was safely gone. But on the other hand, it was only going to get colder, tonight; and who knew how long he planned to stay?

So I scurried across the courtyard, trailing dim shadows in the watery double-moonlight. The roosting chickens paid no more attention to me than they had to Kabir; maybe they were comatose. I entered the church, and, safely inside, removed the finger-sized flashlight I'd secreted in ETHANAC's case. And just for good measure, I patted Hana's silver wristband: *Stay with me, Lady Luck.*

I switched on the flashlight and crossed the chapel where I'd prayed this evening, to the curtained doorway in the opposite wall. And hesitated, at the thought of committing possible sacrilege. The fact that the monks didn't seem to object to Kabir's use of their sacred areas didn't mean that they'd feel the same way about me. After all, as their benefactor, he probably had special dispensations; and as someone out to sabotage him, I probably didn't. But no one could deny that my motives were pure; and so my situational ethics were as justifiable as anyone's—

I pushed aside the hanging and stepped into the inner chamber. There was another doorway in the far wall of this room, also covered. The tapestry was more elaborate, and I realized that that must be the sanctuary which held the sacred relics not even all the monks were allowed to view. I shone the light around the interior of the room I stood in, over manuscripts on dusty tables, over intricately filigreed metal crosses and murals of saints and flat viewscreens on the walls . . . *flat viewscreens*? I pulled the light back.

And there it was. Against the rough surface of the far wall, a rectangular screen just waiting for a chance to speak; a small, neat keyboard console beneath it; a single chair—a computer port. Khorram Kabir's entire empire before me, unguarded and unsuspecting. . . . I stood for a moment limbering up my frozen fingers and letting my fantasies run wild. And then I sat down, and got to work.

The screen bathed the watching saints in an unnatural glow as I switched on the terminal. I plugged ETHANAC's jack into the console, and let him take me mentally by the hand on a journey into this incredible mechanical mind. He started with bits and pieces of code and password he'd sifted from the Xanadu's data banks, posing as an entry of hotel profits to get the system's attention. I wondered offhandedly who actually entered the Xanadu's accounts, since there was no direct linkup; Kabir himself, maybe? Not that it really mattered. . . . ETHANAC began to enter inconsistent data, to call up the system's data-checker, and get a clearer idea of how the system itself functioned. I felt the data-checker emerge, and felt like a social climber getting his first invitation to the grand ball.

But there were still so many worlds-within to conquer: This was probably the largest and most diverse computer net ever created—a veritable heaven of programs within programs like Chinese puzzles, hierarchies of programs, systems, files like a pantheon of strange gods. I wondered what it would feel like to really be a part of that network, to really understand even a fraction of it, and have that fraction become an integral part of myself. . . .

Not this time. I was here to locate a specific subsystem and poke holes in it; I couldn't afford to treat this like a busman's holiday. That could attract attention; and avoiding the attention of the system's gatekeeper routines was one of my main concerns. But ETHANAC's whole "education" had been oriented toward committing just this sort of illegal break-in without tripping the alarms, and if anybody could get us past the electronic beartraps he could. We'd all learned a few things since I blew Big Brother's fuses . . . I wasn't about to wake up any new friends this time, if I could help it.

I sat feeling him sift and poke and discard and try again, probing for one tiny flaw, and then another; holes to let him through from one subroutine to another, getting a little further in, a little higher up, each time. I thought of the Xanadu's outmoded system—getting into that had been as simple as opening a door; getting into this one was like cracking a safe. The process involved thousands of failures for every success; but ETHANAC could try, try again at a rate I physically couldn't comprehend. The subsentient analysis was a strange sensation, faster than thought—I could feel things happen without being aware of how, the way a tennis player hits a ball. Time became formless, the world outside seemed like molasses. It was almost a kind of meditation . . . Zen and the Art of Computer Break-in.

And successfully breaking into this computer network would probably be the greatest achievement of my entire life, in a perverse sort of way:

I'd discovered that by entering the system through this port, I'd chosen the most difficult approach of all. Because the computer itself must be here on Mars—maybe even right in this room . . . there was no time-lag whatsoever. If its mechanical parts were located on Earth, I'd have the advantage only having to deal with its autonomic nervous system, its knee-jerk defense reflexes, which weren't all that flexible. The time-lag would effectively prevent the gatekeepers from getting in my way. But the situation was reversed, and that meant that ETHANAC had met the challenge of a lifetime. Even with only remote-control defenses to protect it, no one had ever gotten into this system successfully from Earth. . . . I wondered whether ETHANAC had just ironically fulfilled the purpose intended by his creators.

This was not only the largest system we'd ever tackled; I was beginning to think it was the strangest system too. It was almost as if I'd programmed it myself . . . and that was no compliment. I'm the solar system's best at finding and correcting bugs, but I have absolutely no sense of programming style. I can't be bothered with it; I go straight for the machine-language basics. Which means that once I've done something, anybody else has a hell of a time untangling my work. They say a camel is a horse put together by a committee—well, I'm a one-man committee; both a blessing and a curse, as my boss once told me. . . . And so was the state of this machine's software. Maybe it had been a security measure: nothing was where it logically belonged, it was buried under piles of unrelated data. It was like creeping through the back rooms of some reclusive trash-fetishist's castle, stacked to the ceiling with junk and old news printouts. And somehow I had to tunnel through it all to the control room, the castle keep, where he kept the supervisor programs that would let me manipulate to my heart's content. . . .

And then, with a sudden rush of triumph, I realized my wish had been granted. Doctors bury their mistakes, and so do programmers, if they're lucky . . . but somebody's luck had just run out. I'd already passed up several obvious errors in the system, because they were just too obvious. But this time I'd found an inconsistency that was utterly inconsequential—and I could use its existence to draw out the supervisor's error-handling routines. They would drop the drawbridge for me, taking me for a Noble Programmer, and I would be *in—*

—deep trouble. Circuits closed, contacts were frozen, the guards moved in on me with swords drawn . . . I'd rung the bell. I'd walked straight into a security trap, and now I was—

Who are you? an incredulous voice demanded.

Going crazy? I shook my head like a stunned cat. *Did I hear—?*

You're trapped, Ethan Ring. You won't escape. I've been waiting for you. . . .

Voices. Now I knew how Joan of Arc felt.

Tell me who and what you are—

My first thought was that I'd inadvertently created another monster, brought this system to life, somehow, too. But I'd never heard *voices.* Even ETHANAC had only been semirational, for his first few hours. . . . "W-who are *you*?" I sub-vocalized the thought, feebly defiant.

I am Khorram Kabir.

So that was it: A megalomaniac computer, believing it was its own creator. . . . .*Or was it—?* Was it possible, could it really be true? Had this crazy-quilt system been sentient all along; had someone actually succeeded in achieving the impossible . . . turning a human mind, or personality, into software—?

Exactly, the self-satisfied voice in my head said; the feel of telepathic speech was like the irritating tickle that catches in your throat and won't let you cough.

So, at last I could put all those rumors to rest. Khorram Kabir wasn't senile, or dead. Oh, no—he was alive and well, and living in a computer. He had literally become a non-person, he had retired from the world and cast off his mortal body in the most genuine sense. His mortal body. . . . If this was Khorram Kabir, then who was that stranger I'd seen tonight—?

As if on cue, a voice behind me said, "Well, Mr. Ring. What a pleasant surprise."

Turning my head at that point was the most difficult thing I'd ever done in my life. Because I already knew that strangled-rabbit voice could only belong to one man. . . . I looked around at him.

For once in my life, why couldn't I have been wrong? Salad stood across the room, helmet in hand, his bald head gleaming like the deadly satisfaction in his eyes.

I leaped up out of the chair, trying to pull ETHANAC's jack free from the panel. But I couldn't get it loose. Kabir had locked it into the console. I stood there tugging at it, the Boy at the Dike with his finger stuck. "Come on, dammit, let go of me!"

Salad leered at me in silent appreciation, and then he pulled out the gun.

I froze, caught with my pants down and my hand in the cookie jar. "I know what this looks like, I knew what you're thinking, but actually I was only—"

The gun spat once, inaudibly, and something hit my knee like an invisible ax. I collapsed into the seat with a cry of heartfelt agony, clutching my leg in disbelief.

"I'm so glad it was you, Mr. Ring," Salad said congenially. "After you betrayed our agreement. After you caused so much damage at the hotel. After you left without paying for any of it. . . ." He broke into a smile that would have done justice to a homicidal maniac. "Well, now you're going to pay for it all, Mr. Ring. Because Mr. Kabir still wants to know who hired you. And I'm going to make you tell me who it was. . . . But please don't tell me too soon; that spoils the fun. And besides, it won't do you a bit of good—" Any minute he was going to be drooling. He lifted the gun again.

"Oh, my God," I moaned, too dazed to think straight. "Oh, my God. Help me, Kabir, please, you don't want to feel him do this to me! Stop him, you can make him stop—!" I don't know where the inspiration came from, but it must have been heaven-sent.

Because the screen in front of me lit up in ten-centimeter letters, "SALAD, STOP."

"Look!" I babbled, patting the screen frantically. "Look, look—"

Salad lowered his gun, and his eyes widened fractionally. They narrowed again. "This is a trick. You tampered—"

"It's no trick!" It's hard to shout through clenched teeth.

"Salad," new lettering, smaller, "this is Kabir." A code sequence printed out. "I want to question this man myself, in my own way. You will not touch him unless I give the order. Understood?"

"But you said—" Salad lowered the gun all the way, looking incredulous. "Understood, sir. I didn't know you could—hear, sir."

"There are a lot of things you don't know about me, Salad," the screen said. "And you never will."

Including the fact that Kabir was reading my mind. . . . *So you throw yourself on my mercy, Ethan Ring?* His electronic telepathy formed words in my mind at the speed of thought; the screen went blank.

Yes, Mr. Kabir, I thought dutifully. *Thank you, sir.* If my voice could have shaken, it would have.

It's a long time since I've—felt pain, Ring. I had forgotten how much I disliked it. . . .

You're not the only one. I glanced down at my soggy pants leg, and wondered if he wanted to remember how it felt to be violently ill. *ETHANAC, help me out—* I felt a slight buzz begin inside my head as he damped out the pain receptors. *Whew* . . . my mind began to clear, *that's got it.*

And we're back to my first question, which you still haven't answered, Ring: Who are you, and what are you? Are you man, or machine? I've never had contact with something like you before. I didn't know such a creature even existed.

The feel of the conscious thought, I realized, was Arabic. I switched into it ingratiatingly. *It's mutual, sir. And I'm both. A man sitting at your terminal, a machine plugged into it: a mind made up of both.* I made my three-color analogy for him.

A true symbiosis! How did it happen? Who made you what you are? Tell me about yourself— I felt a peculiarly poignant eagerness fill my mind.

It all started about a year ago. . . . And for the second time in a couple of days I found myself taking a trip down memory lane, at the behest of an offer I couldn't refuse. . . . *And I came to Mars as a crate of bologna. I've worked here in the Arab territories about a year, doing software maintenance.*

Naturally. I swear there was a chuckle. *Now, tell me how you come to be in your present fix—*

I jammed the memory with a burst of static, before he could read too much. *Sorry. That's classified.*

I can make you tell me. Or Salad can—

Oh, no— I glanced at Salad, waiting there like a vulture, complete with shiny skull; my panic rose again.

Don't panic, Ring. You're much too interesting to me for me to waste you on such an inconsequential matter. Particularly since you've failed at whatever it was you were trying to do to me.

Relief and then dismay replaced my incipient horror. I had failed, ETHANAC had failed, this system had been too smart for us. I wondered whether ETHANAC would have won, if he'd been joined to the superior human mind that should have been his partner. . . . It left me feeling oddly dizzy and drained. Something warm and wet was collecting down inside my right boot. *Thanks, I think.*

You fascinate me, Ring. And you fill me with envy.

I do?

Yes. There are some things even I can't control. You have the five things I can never buy, with all my wealth—the five human senses. I can't really see you, or anything else. I can't hear or touch or taste or smell. And I can't go back . . . my body is dead and buried. This is the closest I've come—this brief sharing of your own senses—to the outside world in thirteen years. Allah, you don't know how much it means to me to have discovered that you exist! And you're the only one?

The only one I know of. I was surprised at the emotion that filled me then, especially that it was all my own. I realized how well ETHANAC understood what he was saying.

As I am the only one. The only Khorram Kabir; the man who may live forever. I control an empire . . . but I can't touch it. I can't see my beloved Xanadu—

Then, why? Why did you . . . do this to yourself? Everyone believes you wanted to get away from all that, that you didn't want anything to do with the world anymore.

I was sick, my health was going. But I didn't want to lose control. I became a 'recluse' to set the stage for this transformation—and it was successful. Only Khorram Kabir could control the resources to achieve what I have become. . . . And now that I have it, I'll never give it up, I'll keep control of my empire in a way that no ruler before me ever managed to do!

I fought down the overwhelming flood of raw ambition that tried to swallow me then, the way it had already swallowed a sixth of the people on Earth— *But you'll never see it rain again, or drink the Milk of Paradise, or touch and be touched by a beautiful woman!* . . . I felt the force break and drain away, leaving me weak. I put my hand over my wrist and slumped back in the chair, *Oh, Hana, think of poor Ethan tonight. . . .* I remembered Kabir's presence in my mind, like a voyeur, and tried to control myself. For some reason it was getting hard to keep my mind on the subject, whatever it was . . . *was it Hana—?*

Hana—? Kabir's emotion backed up into my own again, making it suddenly so unbearable that I almost cried . . . or he did. I'd fed emotions into a computer before, but I'd never had them come back at me like this, until I couldn't tell them from my own. I couldn't tell them from my own. . . .

And all at once he wasn't the Master of the World playing blind man's bluff inside my head anymore. He was just a lonely old man shut away in an institution, trying desperately to keep in touch with life. And suddenly I felt very sorry for him, and it was easy to let him see Hana as I'd first seen her, in the black-light glow of the underworld, and in the Peacock Lounge at the Xanadu. And to remember eating and drinking and sharing the rain. . . . *Rain, rain, go away . . . come again some other day. . . .*

Ring! Are you all right?

Huh? I found myself lying face down across the keyboard, trying to remember how it had happened. *Oh . . . sorry.* I pushed myself up with rubber arms, and flopped back in the seat again.

What's the matter with you? It was somewhere between indignant and appalled.

My lower leg was soaking wet. *I think . . . I've sprung a leak.* Which for some reason struck me so funny that I started to laugh. *It's not funny! It's not funny!* And suddenly it wasn't, and the idea of being forced to sit here and reminisce until I bled to death made me feel very cold and frightened.

Forgive me, Ring. I didn't realize . . . I didn't mean for this to happen. This has meant so much to me—

Poor man, I thought thickly. *Poor Khorram Kabir, you poor bastard, you only want what I wanted . . . what we all want . . . freedom, that's all they want; the right to lead their own lives . . . touch each other . . . watch it rain. . . . But you won't let them have what they want . . . and you can't have it either, so what's the point, you poor bastard? How it must hurt to live with so much sadness. . . .* I touched the screen's blind eye maudlinly, leaving a red spot; overwhelmed by misery and regret and not sure whom it belonged to.

Stop it, Ring! For God's sake— It was like a slap in the face.

I jerked awake again, and took a deep breath.

What is it you want of me? Why did you come here?

A keyhole, I thought. *I want to plant a lousy keyhole in your system for somebody,* managing not to remember who. *Some people who want to be free.*

All right, then. Do it.

What?

Do it. I won't stop you.

Was I really hearing that? *Why?*

Because you had pity on me, Ring. . . . Everyone feels sorry for the people a tyrant oppresses. But very few feel sorry for the way he oppresses himself. You felt sorry for us all . . . and for that I am in your debt. You almost make me feel that

such nobility of purpose deserves to be rewarded—
He drew back, like a snapping turtle pulling back into its shell. *But I'm still a businessman, Ring. So I'll make you a deal. You're the only man in the solar system who can give me what I really want. I want to be able to see through your eyes, and I want to find out what kind of man you really are. The keyhole will remain open as long as you come here, once a month, and let me do that.*

I kept my attention focused on the words with a supreme effort of will. *It's a deal! I'll come back; if I ever . . . get out of here alive, that is—*

I'll see that you do. Plant your keyhole.

The system called off its guards, raised its hands, dropped its drawbridges . . . ETHANAC made the changes in less time than it took to think about it. *So simple. . . .*

Goodbye, then, Ring. Or au revoir. *Take care of yourself—you belong to me.* A ghost of a chuckle, and then there was no one in my mind but me.

"SALAD" appeared on the screen again, and the most beautiful words I'd ever seen: "Get Mr. Ring to the hospital immediately."

Salad pushed away from the manuscript table where he'd been perched patiently, and stared at the message, and at me: The chief executioner, who'd just been told the king had outlawed capital punishment. "Yes, Mr. Kabir—"

"'Curfew shall not ring tonight,' Salad." I grinned a sickly imitation of bravado. It took all the strength I had to pull ETHANAC's jack loose from the panel; even though no one was stopping me, this time. I switched off the terminal, leaving us in sudden darkness.

Salad produced a flashlight before I could find

my own, thoughtfully turned it on me as I pulled myself up out of my seat . . . the sort of light they shine into your eyes when they're giving you the third degree. My boot squelched nauseatingly when I put my weight on the injured leg, and the pain level shot up. ETHANAC blanked it out again obligingly, but I wondered whether I was going to do any permanent damage. My head felt like a tethered balloon. "Give me a hand, Salad. I think you've disqualified me from the standing broad jump."

He crossed the room, still using the flashlight to maximum bad effect, and held out his hand. I reached out, took it, and shifted my weight. Salad released his grip with a slight jerk, and let me fall flat on my face.

I slowly untangled myself in the pool of light, and squinted up at him. I couldn't see his expression, which may have been just as well.

"Oh. Sorry, Mr. Ring . . . but I'm afraid I can't help you."

"What do you mean—?" That didn't come out sounding the way I'd intended it to. "Kabir . . . ordered you to help me, damn it!"

"No, Mr. Ring," he said gently. "He told me to take you to the hospital. And I will, if you can get to my 'copter unaided. You see, he also told me not to touch you, unless he said it was all right. And he never did."

"You know that's . . . what he meant!"

"I always obey his orders explicitly. To the letter. That's why he trusts me." The darkness grinned mockingly.

"He's not going to . . . trust you if I'm . . . not here again in a month. He wants to see me—" I tried to get up, without much luck.

"Pathetic, Mr. Ring."

"It's true! Call him . . . ask him—"

"You're wasting time, Mr. Ring. Every minute you sit there objecting you bleed a little more."

It finally sank through my thickening head that that was the whole point of the game. I began to understand the horror behind the term "cat and mouse." I got all the way to my feet this time, using fury as a crutch, and made it past the curtained doorway, through the prayer chapel, to the church entrance.

The distance across the moonlit courtyard to the dome's airlock seemed to stretch like a topologist's nightmare: fifty meters . . . five hundred . . . five thousand. I kept getting lost; or maybe it only seemed that way. There wasn't a sign of another human being now—and that included what followed me, holding a flashlight. I didn't suppose it would do any good to shout for help, even in Ge'ez, under the circumstances. *God helps those who help themselves.*

But we reached the airlock at last, my shadow and I. I was still in the spotlight; too preoccupied now to be embarrassed by the humiliating loss of privacy. And the light reminded me, inadvertently, that I wasn't wearing an 0_2 breather: The monks were an orderly order, and theirs gleamed like a row of little angels beside the airlock's inner door. I stole one without the slightest regret. I turned the wheel on the airlock door, gasping like a fish out of water, and with the last of my strength gave Salad the finger as we stepped inside.

But as the lock cycled, I realized that even my determination to beat him at his own game wasn't going to be enough. I was disassociating, coming apart . . . a dust storm was rising inside my head . . . red dust. . . . The outer door swung open, and the incredible cold of the Martian night hit me like a fist. *ETHANAC! I'm goin' under—catch me. . . .*

IT'S ALL RIGHT, MICHAEL. LET GO: I HAVE YOU. . . . . NO COLD. NO PAIN. DROPPING CIRCULATION TO MAINTENANCE IN UPPER BODY: REDIRECT OXYGEN TO MOBILE LIMBS. SQUINT YOUR EYES. STEP FORWARD, THROUGH THE DOOR. STEP HIGHER! BALANCE. STEP AGAIN . . . AGAIN . . . VEHICLE TO THE LEFT. STEADY . . . COMPENSATE. MOVE YOUR FEET. WATCH SALAD—DON'T LET HIM TRIP YOU. KEEP BREATHING! WAIT: TWO VEHICLES. TWO? WHICH ONE—? "Salad . . . which one!" BUT HE CAN'T HEAR ME. WAIT FOR HIM. WAIT. HE'LL USE THE LIGHT—HANG ON, MICHAEL.

MORE LIGHT: FIGURES, TWO, COMING TOWARD ME. WHO—? NO, DON'T FALL DOWN! BRACE YOUR LEGS. MOVE YOUR FEET. HAVE TO GET PAST THEM. HAVE TO—

"Ring! Is that you, Ring?"

"Salad, drop it! I've got you covered. Drop it!"

VOICES: NTEBE, KRAUS. . . . HOW—? NO, CAN'T STOP, NOT YET. NOT YET . . . ALMOST SAFE.

"Ring, old man! You're all right!" VOICE: NTEBE. "We were afraid we'd come too late—"

"What did you do to him, Salad? What's the matter with him?" VOICE: KRAUS.

" 'Copter . . . get to the 'copter."

"I have no idea, gentlemen. I caught him threatening Mr. Kabir. That's an illegal act. You're aiding a criminal. That's illegal, too." VOICE: SALAD.

"That's a matter of opinion." VOICE: KRAUS.

" 'Copter . . . let go of me–" PANT LEG FROZEN STIFF. LEG NOT RESPONDING. DON'T FALL. DON'T FALL–

"Oops! Hang on, Ring, I've got you." VOICE: NTEBE. HANDS, ARMS, SUPPORT– "Hana's waiting with the 'copter. We'll get you out of here. Come on, Kraus."

"I've got both these guns on you, Salad. Don't try anything stupid." VOICE: TWO-GUN KRAUS.

"For pity's sake, Kraus, will you come on! Give me a hand here; he's a dead weight." VOICE: NTEBE.

"More than you know, hopefully." VOICE: SALAD. "He's failed, you've all failed. FTI will regret this–"

"Having a good law firm means never having to say you're sorry." VOICE: NTEBE. "Goodbye, Salad. Don't think it's been fun."

MORE HANDS. HELICOPTER COMING UP: GOOD, YES. . . . GOOD HANDS. GOOD GUYS. GOOD RIDDANCE, SALAD–

"Ethan. Ethan–" VOICE: TAKHASHI. "Hurry up–watch his head, Basil!" DOOR SEALING. SAFE NOW. RELAX. . . . "What's wrong with him, what happened? I *knew* it, I knew something was wrong. . . . No, you pressurize, get us up out of here, Basil. Watch out for the downdrafts. Ethan's mine, leave him to me. . . . God, he's cold as a witch's tit; turn up the heat, too. And get out the first aid kit, Cephas, we'll–we'll need bandages, when he thaws out. . . . Ethan, can you hear me?"

WARM ARMS TIGHTENING . . . NICE. CABIN PRESSURIZED–BREATHE DEEP, MICHAEL. . . . "No."

"No?" VOICE: TAKHASHI. "Yarrow–?"

"No."

"ETH–ETHANAC?" VOICE: TAKHASHI.

"Yes."

"My God, he's on autopilot." VOICE: NTEBE.

"Are they–coming back, ETHANAC? They are all right–" VOICE: TAKHASHI . . . UNSTEADY.

BLOOD OXYGEN RISING. RESTORE CIRCULATION. . . . INTERFERENCE . . . long tunnels . . . *help . . . hell . . . hello? Where's my body? . . .*

WELCOME BACK, MICHAEL, EVERY*thing's just where it ought to be.* . . . Breathing pure oxygen under normal pressure was as good as a transfusion. "Brr. H-hold me tight . . . and we will be, Lady Luck," I mumbled, clutching my oxygen mask.

"Are you sure that's the computer?" Ntebe leaned across my legs and peered at me. Beyond him I could see Orion dressed in his starry Sunday best, peeking in through the heavy window glass. I couldn't quite grin at him.

"Doesn't matter . . . we all . . . feel the same way about it." I blinked; the frost was melting off my eyelashes and into my eyes. "You've got your keyhole, Ntebe. Salad . . . lost every bet, tonight."

"Wonderful–!" But he glanced down at my leg, and his face turned grimly glum. "And you lost over a liter. . . ."

"Look on . . . the bright side. I'm still half full."

"We did it, then. We actually did it!" Kraus chortled at the controls. "We foiled two of the greatest villains in the solar system! That's an adventure to—"

"Basil," Hana said, blowing gently on my frozen fingers, "shut up."

The rest was silence.

"I'll never play the violin again, you know." I leaned on my cane at the solarium window, watching black smoke from the factory next to the hospital mushroom into the smog-brown polar air.

"You play with your feet?" Hana said.

I turned back thoughtfully. "You mean there's some other way?"

Kraus groaned.

"Who's the patient here, Kraus, you or me? I'm the only one who's supposed to be in pain." I hobbled across to join Hana at one end of the determinedly cheerful red plastic couch.

"A pain in the neck," Kraus grinned at me good-naturedly, from the other end of it.

"Speaking of which, we're still waiting for Salad's legal ax to fall, on FTI, or at least on us. Somehow I don't think he'll have the nerve to try it—" Ntebe raised his eyebrows. Across the room one of the other patients shouted, "Gin!" and tossed down cards. For some reason, none of them would play with me anymore.

"If anybody gets the ax, it'll be the headsman," I said. "And I'm looking forward to delivering the *coupe de grâce*. . . . I don't think Khorram Kabir will be amused at what happened to me after his lights went out."

Hana put a comforting arm around my shoulders. "Khorram Kabir . . . is software. I still can't believe it. It's too incredible."

"Money can buy you anything, if you've got enough of it. Well, maybe not anything. . . ." I shook my head.

"About your—deal with him, Ring." Ntebe looked back at me, hesitated. "I don't feel I have the right to ask this of you, after what you've done for us already, but if you could pay him those—visits—for even a few months. . . ."

"I plan to keep my appointments." I patted ETHANAC, nodding. "I'm not about to let all that trouble go for nothing. And besides, I want to do it. Because I understand what it means, not to be—" I glanced down at the dusty plastic plant in a pot beside me, remembering. *You belong to me, Ring* . . . for a minute I wondered just exactly what Kabir had had in mind when he'd chuckled at that. But, on the other hand—"Besides, how many people get to play the Ghost of Christmas Past to the biggest Scrooge in the system? I may melt his mechanical heart yet."

He brightened. "Maybe you've got something there."

"I hope it's catching."

"My fireship." Hana kissed me on the cheek.

"Please," I said, reddening. "Do that again."

"Well. Yes." Ntebe stood up, clearing his throat. "Come along, Basil. Let's get ourselves a cup of tea, or something, shall we?"

"What? . . . Oh." Kraus stood up with him. "Oh." They went away quietly.

"So tell me," I held out my wrist, when we were alone at last. "What about this silver bracelet, anyway?"

She drew back. "What about it?"

"How did you know I needed you?"

She laughed. "It's a tracer. And anyway, I kept track of Salad. He followed you . . . we followed him."

"But how did you know I needed you *then*?"

The smile turned sly. "You don't really want me to tell you the truth, do you?"

I thought about that.

"I didn't think so." She touched my wrist tenderly, and glanced away.

I leaned back, letting her beautiful face fill my eyes, and said with sudden earnestness, "Do I want you to predict the future—?"

She looked back at me clinically. "Well, speaking strictly as a doctor, I foresee your needing an extended period of bed rest, and some very special treatment—"

"You're not that kind of doctor!"

"It's not that kind of treatment."

Nevertheless, it worked like a charm.

MOTHER AND CHILD

Part 1: The Smith

All day I have lain below the cliff. I can't move, except to turn my head or twitch two fingers; I think my back is broken. I feel as if my body is already dead, but my head aches, and grief and shame are all the pain I can bear. Remembering Etaa . . .

Perhaps the elders are almost right when they say death is the return to the Mother's womb, and in dying we go back along our lives to be reborn. Between wakings I dream, not of my whole life, but sweet dreams of the time when I had Etaa, my beloved. As though it still happened I see our first summer together herding shenn, warm days in fragrant upland meadows. We didn't love each other then; she was still a child, I was hardly more, and for our different reasons we kept ourselves separated from the world.

My reason was bitterness, for I was *neaa,* motherless. The winter before, I had lost my parents to a pack of kharks as they hunted. My mother's sister's family took me in, as was the custom, but I still ached with my own wounds of loss, and was always an outsider, as much from my own sullenness as from any fault of my kin. I questioned every belief, and could find no comfort. Sometimes, alone with just the grazing shenn, I sat and wept.

Until one day I looked up from my weeping to see a girl, with eyes the color of new-turned earth and short curly hair as dark as my own. She stood watching me somberly as I wiped at my eyes, ashamed and angry.

—What do you want? I signed, looking fierce and hoping she would run away.

—I felt you crying. Are you lonely?

—No. Go away. She didn't. I frowned.—Where did you come from, anyway? Why are you spying on me?

—I wasn't spying. I was across the stream, with my shenn. I am Etaa. She looked as if that explained everything.

And it did; I recognized her then. She belonged to another clan, but everyone talked about her: Etaa, her name-sign, meant "blessed by the Mother," and she had the keenest eyesight in the village. She could see a bird on a branch across a field, and thread the finest needle; but more than that, she had been born with the second sight, she felt the Mother's presence in all natural things. She could know the feeling and touch the souls of every living creature, sometimes even predict when rain would fall. Others in the village had the second sight, but not as clearly as she did, and most people thought she would be the next priestess when she came of age. But now she was still a child, minding the flocks, and I wished she would leave me alone. —Your shenn will stray, O blessed one.

Old hurt pinched her sun-browned face, and then she was running back toward the stream.

—Wait! I stood up, startled, but she didn't see my sign. I threw a stone; it skimmed past her through the grass; she stopped and turned. I waved her back, guilty that my grief had made me hurt somebody else.

She came back, her face too full of mixed feeling to read.

—I'm sorry. I didn't mean to make you unhappy too. I'm Hywel. I sat down, gesturing.

Her smile was as sudden and bright as her disappointment, and passed as quickly. She dropped down beside me like a hound, smoothing her striped kilt. —I wasn't showing off . . . I don't *mean* to. . . . Her shoulders drooped; I had never thought before that blessedness could be a burden like anything else. —I just wanted to— Her fingers hesitated in mid-sign. —To know if you were all right. She looked up at me through her long lashes, with a kind of yearning.

I glanced away uncomfortably across the pasture. —Can you watch your shenn from here? They were only a gray-white shifting blot to me, even when my eyes were clear, and now my eyes were blurred again.

She nodded.

—You have perfect vision, don't you? My hands jerked with pent-up frustration. —I wish I did!

She blinked. —Why? Do you want to be a warrior, like in the old tales? Some of our people want to take the heads of the Neaane beyond the hills for what they do to us. I think in the south some of them *have*. Her eyes widened.

The thought of the Neaane, the Motherless ones, made me flinch; we called them Neaane because they didn't believe in the Mother Earth as we did, but in gods they claimed had come down from the sky. We are the Kotaane, the Mother's children, and to be *neaa* was to be both pitiful and accursed, whether you were one boy or a whole people. —I don't want to kill people. I want to be farsighted so I can be a hunter and kill kharks, like they killed my parents!

—Oh. She brushed my cheek with her fingers, to show her sorrow. —When did it happen?

—At the end of winter, while they were hunting.

She leaned back on her elbows and glanced up into the dull blue sky, where the Sun, the Mother's consort, was struggling to free his shining robes once more from the Cyclops. The Cyclops' rolling bloodshot Eye looked down on us malevolently, out of the wide greenness of her face. —It was the doing of the Cyclops, probably,

Etaa sighed. —Her strength is always greatest at the Dark Noons, big Ugly-face; she always brings pain with the cold! But the Mother sees all—

—The Mother didn't see the kharks. She didn't save my parents; She could have. She gives us pain too, the Great Bitch!

Etaa's hands covered her eyes; then slowly they slid down again. —Hywel, that's blasphemy! Don't say that or She will punish you. If She let your parents die, they must have offended Her. She lifted her head with childish self-righteousness.

—My parents never did anything wrong! Never! My mind saw them as they always were, bickering constantly. . . . They stayed together because they had managed to have one child, and though they'd lost two others, they were fertile together and might someday have had a fourth. But they didn't like each other anyway, and maybe their resentment was an offense. I hit Etaa hard on the arm and leaped up. —The Mother is a bitch and you are a brat! May you be sterile!

She gasped and made the warding sign. Then she stood up and kicked me in the shins with her rough sandals, her face flushed with anger, before she ran off again across the pasture.

After she was gone I stood throwing rocks furiously at the shenn, watching them run in stupid terror around and around the field.

And because of it, when I had worn out my rage, I discovered one of my shenn had disappeared. Searching and cursing, I finally found the stubborn old ewe up on the scarp at the field's end. She was scrabbling clumsily over the ragged black boulders, cutting her tender feet and leaving tufts of her silky wool on every rock and thorn bush. I caught her with my crook at last and dragged her back down by her flopping ears, while she butted at me and stepped on my bare feet with her claws out. I cursed her mentally now, not having a hand to spare, and cursed my own idiocy, but mostly I cursed the Mother Herself, because all my troubles seemed to come from Her.

Scratched and aching all over, I got the ewe down the crumbling hill to the field at last, whacked her with my crook, and watched her trot indignantly away to rejoin the flock. I started toward the stream to wash my smarting body, but Etaa was ahead of me, going down to drink. Afraid that she would see me for the fool I was, I threw myself down in the shade of the hillside instead and pretended to be resting. I couldn't tell if she was even looking at me, though I squinted and stretched my eyes with my fingers.

But then suddenly she was on her feet running toward me, waving her arms. I got up on my knees, wondering what crazy thing—

And then a piece of the hill gave way above me and buried me in blackness.

I woke spitting, with black dirt in my eyes, my

nose, my mouth, to see Etaa at my side still clawing frantically at the earth and rubble that had buried my legs. All through her life, though she wasn't large even among women, she had strength to match that of many men. And all through my life I remembered the wild, burning look on her face, as she turned to see me alive. But she didn't make a sign, only kept at her digging until I was free.

She helped me stand, and as I looked up at the slumped hillside the full realization of what had been done came to me. I dropped to my knees again and rubbed fistfuls of the tumbled earth into my hair, praising Her Body and begging Her forgiveness. Never again did I question the Mother's wisdom or doubt Her strength. I saw Etaa kneel beside me and do the same.

As we shared supper by my tent, I asked Etaa how she'd known when she tried to warn me. —Did you see it happening?

She shook her head. —I *felt* it, first . . . but the Mother didn't give me enough time to warn you.

—Because She was punishing me. She should have killed me for the things I thought today!

—But it was me who made you angry. It was my fault. I shouldn't have said that about your parents. It was awful, it was—cruel.

I looked at her mournful face, shadowed by the greening twilight. —But it was true. I sighed. —And it wasn't just today that *I* have cursed the Mother. But I'll never do it again. She must have been right, to let my parents die. They hated staying together; they didn't appreciate the blessing of their fertility, when others pray for children but can't make any.

—Hywel . . . maybe they're happier now, did

you ever think? She looked down self-consciously. —To return to the Mother's Womb is to find peace, my mother says. Maybe She knew they were unhappy in life, so She let them come back, to be born again.

—Do you really think so? I leaned forward, not knowing why this strange girl's words should touch me so.

She wrinkled her face with thought. —I really think so.

And I felt the passing of the second shadow that had darkened my mind for so long, as though for me it was finally Midsummer's Day and I stood in the light again.

Etaa insisted on staying with me that night; her mother was a healer, and she informed me that I might have "hidden injuries," so gravely that I laughed. I lay awake a long time, aching but at peace, looking up past the leather roof into the green-lit night. I could see pallid Laa Merth, the Earth's Grieving Sister, fleeing wraithlike into the outer darkness in her endless effort to escape her mother, the Cyclops, who always drew her back. The Cyclops had turned her lurid Eye away from us, and the shining bands of her robe made me think for once of good things, like the banded melons ripening in the village fields below.

I looked back at Etaa, her short dark curls falling across her cheek and her bare chest showing only the softest hint of curves under her fortune-seed necklace. I found myself wishing that she would somehow magically become a woman, because I was just old enough to be interested; and then suddenly I wished that then she would have me for her man, something I'd never thought about anyone else before. But if she were a woman, she would become our priestess and have her pick of men and not want one without the second sight. . . . I remembered the look she'd given me as she dug me out of the landslide, and felt my face redden, thinking that maybe I might have a chance, after all.

Through the summer and the seasons that followed I spent much time with Etaa and slowly got used to her strange skills. I had never known what it was like to feel the Mother's touch, or even another human's, on my own soul; and since I had few close friends, I didn't know the ways of those who had the second sight. To be with Etaa was to be with someone who saw into other worlds. Often she started at nothing, or told me what we'd find around the next turn of the path; she even knew my feelings sometimes, when she couldn't see my face. She felt what the Earth feels, the touch of every creature on Her skin.

Etaa's second sight made her like a creature of the forest (for all animals know the will of the Mother), and, solitary like me, she spent much time with only the wild things for company. Often she tried to take me to see them, but they always bolted at my coming. Etaa would wince and tell me to move more slowly, step more softly, breaking branches offends the Earth . . . but I could never really tell what I was doing wrong.

The next year on Midsummer's Eve I was initiated into manhood. During the feast that followed, while I sat dripping and content after my ducking in the sacred spring, Etaa sat proudly at my side. But when midnight came I left the celebration to walk in the fields with Hegga, because for that one could only ask a woman, and

Etaa was still a child. Which she proved, by sticking her tongue out at Hegga as we passed. But it made me smile, since it meant she was closer to being a woman, too.

Now that I was a man, Teleth, who was the village smith, asked me to be his apprentice. Smithing is a gift of the Sun to the Fire clan, and a man of that clan is always the smith, whatever clan he marries into. Teleth, my mother's cousin, had a son who would have followed him, but his son was farsighted, and not much good at the close work smithing required. I was Teleth's closest nearsighted kin; but he signed that I was good with my hands and quick with my mind too, which pleased him more. And pleased me too, more than I could tell him; because besides the honor, it meant that I'd have a better chance of impressing Etaa.

Though she was still a child, whenever I saw her passing in the village, or watched her sign to the people who came to see her, the grace of her manner and her words left me amazed; especially since for me words never came easy, and my hands showed my feelings better by what they made from metal and wood. But often I saw her, from the smithy, going off alone on the path to the Mother's Glen, and I remembered the burden she always carried with her, and how she had lightened mine. And then I'd go back to work, and work twice as hard, hoping Teleth would take pity on me and let me go early.

But usually Teleth kept me working every spare minute; he was young, but he had a lung sickness that made him cough up blood, and he was afraid he wouldn't live long. When I could be with Etaa at last, my hands tangled with excitement while I tried to set free the things I could never share with anyone else. With me Etaa was free to be the child she couldn't be with anyone else; and though sometimes it annoyed me, and I thought she would never grow up, I endured it, because I saw it was something she needed; and because she would pull my head down and kiss me sometimes as lightly as the touch of a rainbow fly, before she ran away.

We were always together at the Four Feasts and for other rituals, because until she became a woman she wouldn't be our priestess. We saw each other in the fields at planting and harvest too, when everyone worked together, and sometimes in the summer she'd come foraging and berry picking with me. Having eyes that saw both near and far, she could choose whatever task she liked; and, she said, she liked to be with me.

Usually our berry picking went crazy with freedom, and more berries got eaten and stepped on than ever went into our baskets. But one windless, muggy day in the second summer after my initiation, we went in search of red burrberries and Mother's moss for healing. All through the morning Etaa was strangely reserved and solemn, as though she were practicing her formal face in front of me now too. I tried to draw her out, and when I couldn't, I began to feel desperate at the thought that I'd offended her by something I didn't know I'd done—or worse, that she was finally losing interest in me.

—Mother's Tits! I jerked back from a thorn, cursing and fumbling all at once, and lost another handful of berries.

Etaa looked back from the stream bank, where

she was peeling up moss, sensing sharp emotions as she always did. —Hywel, are you all right?

I nodded, barely able to make out her signs from where I stood. —Just save some of that moss for me. I'm being stabbed to death.

She came scrambling up the bank. —Let me pick, then, and you get the moss. It will soothe your hands while you work.

—I'm all right. I felt my old sullenness rise up in me.

—I don't mind. My scratches are better already . . . Look! There's a rubit. It's the Mother's bird; She wants you to change places with me.

—How do you know what it means? You're not the priestess yet. I squinted along her pointing finger. —And that's not a rubit, it's a follower bird.

—Yes, it is a rubit, I can feel its—

—It is not! I crossed my arms.

—Hywel— She stared at me. —What's wrong with you today?

—What's wrong with *you*? All day you've acted like you barely know me! I turned away, to hide the things my face couldn't.

At last she touched my shoulder; I turned back, to see her blushing as red as the burrberries and her hands twitching at her waist. —I didn't mean to . . . but I couldn't tell you . . . I thought . . . Oh, Hywel, will you walk in the fields with me on Midsummer's Eve? Her face burned even redder, her eyes as bright as the Sun.

Laughter burst out of me, full of relief and joy. I caught her up in my arms and swung her, my body saying *yes* and *yes* and *yes*, while she hung on and I felt her laugh her own relief away. I set her down, and straightened the links of my belt to cover my speechlessness. Then I looked her over, grinning, and signed, —So, brat, you've finally grown up?

She stretched her face indignantly. —I certainly have. So please don't call me "brat" anymore. As a matter of fact, my mother hasn't cut my hair for nearly six months, and you never even noticed!

I touched the dark curls that reached almost down to her shoulders now. —Oh. I guess I didn't. I'll have to make you a headband, to go with your necklace.

Her hand rose to the string of jet and silver beads I had made for her. —My necklace doesn't hang straight anymore, either.

—I noticed that. I grinned again, moving closer.

She caught my head and pulled it down to kiss me, as she always did; but this time she didn't pull away, and her kiss was more like fire than a rainbow fly's wing.

I jerked away instead. —Hai, I never taught you that! Who have you been with?

—Nobody. Hegga told me you liked that! She danced away, and hands waving wildly, slipped and fell down the bank into the bed of moss.

I leaped down the bank after her, landing beside her in the soft, gray-green moss. —Gossip about me, will you? I signed. And then I taught her a few things Hegga hadn't told her about.

It seemed to me that Midsummer's Eve would never come. But it came at last, and I found myself laying my cape out on the soft earth between the rows of wheat. I drew Etaa down beside me, her woman's tunic still clinging wetly against her. And then we made love together for the first time, asking fertility for the fields and for ourselves, while I wondered if I was dreaming, because I'd dreamed it often enough.

After, we lay together in the gentle warm night, seeing each other's smiles bathed in green glow, watching the Cyclops like a great striped melon overhead. I gave her the earrings I'd made for her, silver bells shaped like winket blossoms, the symbol of a priestess of the Mother. She took them almost with awe, stroking them with her fingers, and signed that they had a beautiful soul. And I thought of how she would become our priestess tomorrow on Midsummer's Day, and pulled her close again, wondering what would happen between us then. Etaa wiggled her hands free, and asked if she was really a woman now, in my eyes. I kissed her forehead and signed, –In every way, feeling her heart beating hard against me. And then, proudly, as if she had read my mind, she asked me to be her husband. . . .

We didn't return to the village until dawn; and the harvest that year was bountiful.

But cold drizzling rain falls now, the sky is gray with grief, I lie below the cliff and even yesterday is beyond the reach of my crippled hands. Only yesterday . . . yesterday Midsummer's Day came again, the Day of Fruitfulness, the greatest of the Mother's sacred feasts–and the day that should have been our joy, Etaa's and mine. Yesterday our Mother Earth escaped the shadow of the envious Cyclops, and was united again with her shining lover the Sun, once more defying darkness and barren night. And yesterday the priestess of our village took the Mother's part in ritual, and a man of the appointed clan was her consort, to ensure a safe passage through the seasons of Dark Noons and a better future for our people. Because the priestess of a village is the woman most blessed by the Mother, each Midsummer's Day by tradition she joins with a man of a different clan, in celebration, and in the hope of creating a child blessed as she is, who will strengthen the blood of its father's clan.

This year, as in the past seven years, Etaa was our priestess; but this year my own clan had chosen her consort, and they had chosen me. Etaa's face mirrored my own joy when I told her; because though I was smith now, and though I was her husband, that highest honor usually went to the clansman most gifted with the second sight.

And then on Midsummer's Day Etaa shook me awake at dawn, her eyes filled with love. She wore only her shift, and already her Midsummer garlands twined in the wild dark curls of her hair. She smelled of summer flowers. —Hywel, it's Midsummer!

I felt myself laugh, half a yawn. —I know, I know, priestess! I could hardly forget—

—Hywel, I have a surprise. She glanced down suddenly, and her hands trembled as she signed. I saw her silver earrings flash in the light. —I missed my monthly time, and I think—I think—

—Etaa! I touched her stomach, still flat and firm beneath the thin linen of her shift.

—Yes! Her smile broke into laughter as I pulled her down beside me into the hammock. Eight years of marriage and seven Midsummer's Days had passed, and we had begun to think Etaa was barren, like so many others; until now—

I held her tightly in the soft clasp of our hammock, swaying gently side by side. —We're truly blessed, Etaa. Maybe the Mother was waiting for this day. I began to kiss her, pulling at her shift, but all at once she pushed me away.

—No, Hywel, today we have to wait!

I grinned. —You take me for an old man, me, the father of your child? I won't slight the Mother today—but neither will I slight my wife!

Yesterday was all it could have been, the Sun's glory dazzling the sky, the bright fields of grain . . . Etaa's radiant face in the Mother's Glen, on the day when she became Wife and Mother to us all, and I was her chosen.

But then, this morning, she asked me to let her ride with us when I went to trade with the Neaane. We have traded with the Neaane since we first settled on their border, longer ago than anybody can remember. They are a strange, inward people who have lost all understanding of the Mother. Their lives are grim and joyless because of it; they even persecute their people who are blessed with the second sight, calling them witches. They believe in gods who live in the sky, who abandoned them, and, they say, caused the plague that took the Blessed Time from all people.

We never liked their beliefs, but we liked their possessions: soft-footed palfers to carry burdens or pull a plow, new kinds of seed for our fields—even a way to keep the fields fertile over many years, which gave us a more settled life. They wanted our metalwork and jewelry, and the hides of wild animals, because they like to show wealth even more than we do, especially the ones who have most of it. Settled farming has given them time to develop many strange customs, including setting some people above all others, often for no good reason as far as we could see, not wisdom or courage or even good vision.

Still, our trade was good for both of us, and so

we lived together in peace until, in the time the elders still remember, the Neaane's gods returned to them—or so they believed. With the gods' return the Neaane turned against us, saying it proved their beliefs were the only truth, and we, the Kotaane, were an abomination to their gods. Ugly rumors had come to the village of incidents farther south, and even here ill-feeling hurt our dealings with the local lord and his people at Barys-town. I didn't want to see it grow into war, because I had never wanted to kill anyone, and because a war with the powerful Neaane could only bring us death and pain. I also didn't want to expose my priestess-wife with her unborn child to the hostility and insults I'd gotten used to in Barys-town. But she insisted, saying she wanted adventure; she was as irresistible as the summer day, and as beautiful, and I gave in, because I wanted to share it with her.

When we reached Barys-town, we found it choked with the soldiers of the king, the most powerful lord in their land. He was making a rare visit to his borderlands, probably to make certain they were secure against us. I saw the king himself, not thirty feet away but hardly more than a blur to my eyes; he sat on his sharp-footed horse, watching with his nobles as we began to barter. But then his soldiers crowded around us, waving at Etaa and mocking her, calling her "witch" and "whore." One tried to pull her from her palfer, but she hit him with an iron pot. The king made no sign to stop them, and angrily I ordered my goods taken up, not caring who my nervous palfer stepped on in the crowd. I had taken too many insults from the people of Barys-town in the past, and while they gathered sullenly around I told them this insult to my wife was the last one, and they would get no more metal from me. We turned and rode away, passing the fat local priest of the sky-gods, who had come for the jeweled god-sign he had commissioned from me. Seeing him, I threw it onto a dunghill. I didn't look back to see whether he ran to fetch it out. Etaa was very pale, riding beside me; she signed that it was an evil place behind us, and begged me to keep my promise and never go back, because she'd seen hatred in too many eyes.

Then horror froze her face, though I didn't see anything; she turned in her saddle, looking wildly back at the town. —Hywel!

My palfer lunged sideways as an arrow struck its flank. I jerked its head back, saw the mounted men coming fast behind us, the sunlight sparking on chain mail. Etaa pulled at my arm and we kicked our palfers into a gallop, getting drenched with spray as we plunged through the stream that crossed the trail.

We rode for the hills that separated our village from the Neaane, hoping to lose the soldiers in the rough brush where our palfers were surer-footed. But the Neaane seemed to know our every move; again and again we lost sight of them, but they never lost us, and always they cut us off from escape. We knew nothing about the broken uplands, soon we were lost and scattered until only Etaa and I still rode together; but the soldiers followed like hounds on a trail.

Until at last the rigid black-striped hands of a stream-cut gorge brought us to the end of our run—the edge of a cliff where the snow water dashed itself down, down to oblivion, and there was nowhere left to go. My palfer sank to its knees as I slid from its back and went to look down. The drop was sheer, a hundred feet or more onto the wet-silvered rocks below. I turned back, stunned with despair. —They still follow?

—Yes! Etaa threw herself off her palfer, her dappled gown mud-smeared, the summer blossoms torn from her hair. She clung to me, breathing hard, and then turned back to face the brush-filled gorge. —Mother, they're coming, they still come! How can they follow us, when they can't *see*? She trembled like a trapped beast. —Why, Hywel? Why are they doing this?

I touched her cheek, bloody with scratches, with my own scratched hand. —I don't know! But . . . My hands tried to close over the words. —But you know what they'll do, if they take us.

Her eyes closed. —I know . . . Her arms closed in fear around her body.

—And burn us alive then, so that our souls can never rest. I glanced toward the cliff, trembling now too. —Etaa— Her eyes were open again and following my gaze.

—Must we— Her hands pressed her stomach, caressed our child.

I saw the riders now, a shifting blur down the shadowed canyon. —We have to; we can't let them take us.

We went together to the cliff's edge and stood looking down, clinging together, dizzy with the drop and fear. Etaa threw out a quick handful of dirt and prayed to the Mother, as it drifted down, that She would know and receive us. And then she looked up at me, shaking so that I could barely understand her. —Oh, Hywel, I'm so afraid of heights . . . Her mouth quivered; she might have laughed. She drew my head down then and we kissed, long and sweetly. —I love you only, now and always.

—Now and always— I signed. I saw in her eyes that there was no more time. —Now! I fumbled for her hand, seeing soldiers at the mouth of the gorge, her stricken face, and then—nothing. I leaped.

And felt her hand jerk free from mine at the last instant. I saw her face fall upward, framed in dark hair, through cold rushing eternity; and then my body smashed on the rocks below, and tore the bitter anguish from my mind.

Why I ever woke again at all I don't know; or why I still live now, when I would gladly die and be done with my pain. But I woke into nightmare, trapped in this broken body with my shame: knowing I had jumped and Etaa had not. I had let her be taken by the Neaane. I tortured my eyes for some sign, some movement above the face of the black-striped cliff; but there was nothing, only the glaring edge of day, the red Eye of the Cyclops. Etaa was gone. The falling river leaped and foamed beside me, mocking my grief and my aching mouth with cold silver drops. I strained my head until my metal collar cut into my throat, but nothing moved. And so I lay still finally, and prayed, half in dreams and half in madness, and couldn't even form her name: Etaa, Etaa . . . forgive me.

Overhead the clouds gathered purple-gray, darkening the noon; the Mother in Her grief drew Her garments close and rejected Her Lover. The crops will fail. She has cursed Her children for this abomination; for the unbearable sacrilege of the Neaane, for the pitiful weakness of Hywel,

Her Lover and son. She tears the clouds with knives of light, crying vengeance, and Her tears fall cold and blinding on my face. I drown in Her tears, I drown in sorrow . . . Mother! If I could move one more finger, to make Your sign . . . Giver of Life, let me live! Give me back my body, and I will give You the heads of the Neaane. I will avenge this desecration, avenge Your priestess . . . my Etaa . . . Mother, hear me—

Who touches my face? Work, eyes, damn you . . . Smiling, because I'm still alive . . . they wear black and red. They are the king's men! And they will take my soul. Mother, let me die first. No. Let me join my Etaa, on the wind. And have pity on us. . . .

Part 2: The King

It's hardly an army fit for a king. . . . But Archbishop Shappistre tells my people openly these days that King Meron is bewitched—and they believe him. They believe anything the Church tells them. My poor people! Though with my only child lost, and the Kedonny eating away Tramaine while the Gods do nothing, who can blame them? But if I angered the Gods by wanting the Kedonny Witch, if I brought myself ruin, it wasn't because my mind was not my own. It was because it was too much my own, and I knew exactly what I was doing.

And yet, when I look back and remember how I came to this, perhaps there was a kind of bewitchment about it. For it was on the day I first saw her that the plan came into my mind, as I watched her ride into the border village with the Kedonny traders: my Black Witch, my Etaa . . . The

Earl of Barys' priest pointed her out to me, signing she was a pagan priestess, his fat hands trembling at how these godless Kedonny worshipped wantonness and *hearing*; at which point he spat religiously. I fumbled for my lenses to get a better look, and was surprised to see, not some debauched crone, but a fresh-faced girl with masses of dark hair falling loose across her shoulders.

The Kedonny believe that hearing is a godly blessing, and not a curse, as our Church considers it to be; and for my own part, all my life I've questioned the practices that teach us to suppress it. Why should any gods who had our best interests in mind ask us to weaken ourselves? Why, when my own father had passing good vision, had he felt guilty about it, and chosen for my mother a woman who could barely see his face—so that without the lenses so kindly presented me by the Gods, I must stumble into doorframes in a most unkingly manner? Now, watching the Kedonny priestess, revered as the most gifted of her people, my old discontent was transformed. Suddenly I realized that my own heirs didn't need to suffer the same weakness and dependency. I would get them a mother who could give them the strengths I could not. . . .

I snapped out of my thoughts to see the Kedonny traders riding abruptly away, their faces set in anger, while my men-at-arms gestured curses and the villagers shuffled sullenly between them. Almost without thinking, I summoned my carriage and gave orders to my men for pursuit.

As my carriage rose into the air over the heads of the gaping locals, I looked down on the earl's priest digging inexplicably in a dunghill. If I were a religious man, I might have taken it for a sign.

My carriage was made by the Gods, a smooth sphere with a texture like ivory that not only moved over land without using palfers but could take to the sky like a bird. From the air I could track the fleeing Kedonny easily, and guide my men in separating the woman from the rest—all except one man, who stayed stubbornly at her side even when we drove them into a trap. But in the end he was no problem, because he flung himself from the cliff, apparently afraid of being burned alive. I saw his body smashed on the rocks below, and turned away with a shudder, thinking how close I had come to losing what I sought—for my men said that the woman had pulled back from the edge at the last second, and they had barely gotten to her in time. Some of them had thrown her down on the ground, with obvious intent, and I disciplined those with the flat of my sword, in a fury edged with shame. Then I took her up myself, her face the color of hearth ash, and carried her to my carriage.

Being king, I had no need to explain my behavior to anyone at Barys Castle, though there was a flutter of knowing amusement among the nobles as I said an early good-night. I went directly to my chambers, where the Kedonny priestess waited, and left orders with my watch that they were not to disturb me.

The woman sat huddled at the window slit, staring out into the sodden twilight; but as I entered she jerked around, fixing her wide, burning eyes on me. I smiled, because it proved she could hear, and because I saw again that she was a beauty. But seeing me, she pressed back against the cold stone slit as though she wanted to throw herself out.

"Your lover is dead—"

She hesitated, her face blank, and I realized she couldn't read lips. I repeated with my hands, —Your lover is dead. You tried to follow him, and failed. I wouldn't try it again.

She understood the common sign-speech at least, for she sank back down on the seat with her face in her hands. I brought my own hands together sharply, and she glanced up again, startled. I noticed a meal, untouched, on my carven chest beside her. —Will you eat?

She shook her head, her face still frozen.

—Stand up.

She rose stiffly, her hands clutching at her torn gown, her slender arms bare except for bracelets and burned as dark as any peasant's. Her unbound hair gleamed black in the flickering firelight, tangled with wilting flowers and twigs. On her face the dust of flight was smeared and tracked by tears, but I was relieved to see she wasn't the dirt-encrusted barbarian I had half expected; she looked cleaner than some members of my own court. Her ragged dress was coarsely woven and dull-colored, but somehow it brought to my mind the pattern of green leaves and the muted light of deep woods. . . . This was my wanton priestess, the fertile Earth incarnate, who would strengthen the royal line. And even now her witchy beauty went to my head like wine.

It must have shown, for she shrank back again. I pulled off my cloak, amused. —What, priestess, am I so hard to look at? They say a Kedonny priestess will lie with any man who wants her. I touched my crown. —Well, I'm king in this land; surely that makes me as good as any Kedonny shennherd. I caught her arms, and suddenly she came to life, fighting with a strength that stunned me. She struck at my face, knocking off my lenses, and I felt more than saw them shatter on the floor. Angry, I dragged her to the bed and threw her down, pulling off the rags of her dress.

And then I forced her, ruthlessly, in the way I thought befitted a whore of the uncivilized Kedonny. On the bed she did not struggle, but lay limp as a corpse under me, biting her lips while fresh tears of humiliation ran down her face, staining the satin pillows. Her eyes were as brown as peat, the only part of her that showed life, and they tore at me in grief and outrage and supplication. But I looked away, too angry and too eager to admit I had no right to make her mine.

And whatever else may come to pass, that is the one thing I will never forgive myself. Because I did not use a pagan slut that night: I raped a gentle woman, on the day she saw her husband die. Because later I came to love her; but I could never undo the wrong, or hope to change the bitterness I had caused in her heart.

She slept far into the next day, the sleep of exhaustion; but she sat waiting, clad in her rags, when I came back to my chamber after making ready for our departure. She looked as if she hadn't slept at all, or as if she had wakened to find herself still caught up in a nightmare. But she lifted her hands and made the first words I had seen from her, strangely accented: —Will you let me go now?

It took me a moment to realize that she thought I had done all this merely for a night's pleasure. —No. I'm taking you with me to Newham.

—What do you want of me? Her hands trembled slightly.

I pushed my new lenses higher on my nose. —I want your child.

Her hands pressed her stomach in an odd gesture of fear, then leaped into a series of words that meant nothing to me; I guessed she was pleading with me in her own language.

I shook my head and signed patiently, —I want you to bear me sons. I want your—your "blessings" for them. They will be princes, heirs to the throne of Tramaine. They'll have luxuries you can't imagine—and so will you, if you obey me.

She twisted away hopelessly to gaze out the window slit. I could see the line of hills that separated us from the Kedonny, gray land merging into gray sky in the silver rain. Her hands pressed her stomach again.

I clapped and she looked back at me. —What is your sign, priestess?

—Etaa.

—The serving women will bring you new clothes, Etaa. My fingers tangled on the unfamiliar word. —We leave within the hour.

We returned to the palace at Newham, since continuing in the marches would only have made an incident likely; our return took several days, because my carriage had to go more slowly than usual for the sake of my retinue. But we outdistanced the rain at last, and though the roads were mired, the fresh rolling green of the land, the fertile fields and dappled groves of horwoods filled me with pride. Looming Cyclops, which the peasants called the Godseye, merged its banded greens with the green of the earth, and to one side I could see the gibbous outer moon paled by its magnificence. The outer moon was swirled with white that the court astronomer said was clouds, like the ones on Earth. When I was young I had thought of taking the Gods' carriage and flying out to see it, having been told that men once lived there too. But the Gods said the air grew thin as you went higher, and told me I would suffocate if I tried. I tried anyway, and found they were right.

The Kedonny woman accepted the matter of flight without the terror I had expected, only asking, —How does it do this?

—The Gods give it power. It was a gift to my grandfather on their return to Earth.

—There are no gods; there is only the Goddess. A small defiance flickered on her face.

I glanced briefly at the forward compartment, where my coachman tended our flight. —I agree: there are no Gods. But never say it again, priestess, since you know well enough what happens to heretics. You're under my protection, but my archbishop will not welcome a pagan at court.

She settled back into the velvet cushions, and into her quiet resignation, confined and incongruous in the stiff, brocaded gown and the modesty of her headdress. Small silver bells shaped like winket blossoms dangled from wires piercing her ears; she toyed with them constantly. Sometimes as she did she would almost smile, her eyes fixed on nothing.

As I watched her, the image came to me of a pitiful wild child I had seen as a boy, kept in a cage at a fair. The kharks had stolen human children and raised them as their own, until the Gods came and destroyed the kharks. The wild humans could never adjust to normal life again, and I had wondered if there was something about being wild that was better than being a prince, and it saddened me to think that all the kharks were gone. I looked away from Etaa, falling into another memory of my childhood and the Gods: of the time I had inadvertently spied on them during hide-and-hunt with the pages—and seen the grotesque, inhuman thing they treated as a brother. And somehow I knew that this *thing* was the Gods' true form, and that the too-perfect faces they showed to us were only enchantments. I slipped away and ran to tell my father, but he was furious at my blasphemy, and beat me for it, forbidding me ever to speak against our Gods again. I never did, for I realized quickly enough that whatever they weren't, they had powers even a king dared not question. I often wondered if my father had realized that too. But privately I never gave up my heresies, and because of that I found less and less that was deserving of reverence in the teachings of the Church. Which is why my cousin, Archbishop Shappistre, and I have never been much in accord. Why, indeed, he would gladly see me dead and damned.

The archbishop was quick to inform me of his displeasure in the latest instance, after my arrival at the palace at Newham. My good wife, the queen, did not come out to meet us, sending word that she was indisposed. I wondered if she had heard that I was bringing back a mistress; but since through fifteen years of marriage she had rarely been disposed to come and greet me, it hardly mattered. I espied her brother the archbishop among the nobles, however, marking my progress across the banner-bright courtyard from the carriage, with Etaa at my side. He alone was not amused; but then, like his sister, he rarely was. I anticipated a visit from him before the day was out.

I was not disappointed, for early in the evening my watchman entered the room, standing patiently with his face to the door until I should happen to notice and acknowledge him. Etaa started at his entrance, and I caught her motion in the mirror I had fixed at the side of my lenses; it occurred to me that her very presence could be a useful thing. I went to touch the watchman's shoulder, giving him audience, and was informed that the archbishop desired to speak with me. I sent for him, and returned to the table where I was laboriously reviewing the reports sent to me by my advisers. Etaa watched from the long bench where she befriended the fire, avoiding me. Even though she did, after so many years alone I found that the constant presence of a woman was oddly comforting.

The archbishop did not appear to share my feelings, however. His gaunt, ascetic face had always seemed at odds with the flaming richness of his robes; but the look of pious indignation that he affected on seeing Etaa touched on the absurd. "Your majesty." The modish sleeves of his outer robe swept the flags as he bowed low. "I had hoped I might speak with you—alone."

I smiled. "Etaa does not read lips, my lord. You may speak freely in her presence." I gained a certain pleasure at his discomfort, having been made uncomfortable by him often enough in my youth . . . and more recently.

"It is about—this woman—that I've come to your majesty. I strongly protest her presence at court; it's hardly fitting for our king to take a pagan priestess for a leman. Indeed, it smacks of blasphemy." I fancied seeing hungry flames leap behind his eyes; or perhaps it was only firelight reflecting on his lenses. "The Gods have expressed their displeasure to me. And the queen, your lawful wife, is extremely upset."

"I daresay the queen, your sister, has little reason to be upset with me. I have allowed her all the lovers she wants, and the Gods know she has enough of them."

The archbishop stiffened. "Are you saying she is not within her right?"

"Not at all." Divorce was forbidden by the Church, which places duty far above pleasure. As a result, it was common that childless couples would seek an heir from formalized liaisons; though most of the queen's were far from being that. "But we were married, as you know, when I was sixteen, and in all the years since she has not produced a child. If I couldn't give her one, I would gladly acknowledge someone else's. But she is ten years my senior—frankly, my lord, I've begun to give up hope." I didn't add that I'd even given up trying—our marriage had been arranged to bind factions, and it had never been a love match. "This woman pleases me, and I must have an heir. Her beliefs will not affect her childbearing."

"But she is not of noble breeding—"

"She is not a Shappistre by blood, you mean? You would do well to contemplate the scriptures and the law, my lord. The relationship between church and state is a two-edged blade; take care that you don't cut yourself on it."

He bowed low again, his bald head reddening to match his jeweled cap. "Your majesty . . ." Abruptly he glanced at Etaa and clapped his hands. Etaa, who had returned to her fire-watching, started visibly and turned. A smile of triumph crossed his face. —She hears. I must request that your majesty have her ears put out as soon as possible . . . in accordance with the scriptures, and the law. His hands moved carefully in the common signing.

My fists clenched over an angry retort. Then, evenly and also by hand, I replied, —She is a foreigner. While under my protection she is subject to neither the religion nor the laws of Tramaine. And now, good night, Archbishop; I am very weary after my long journey. I crossed my arms.

My archbishop turned without another word and left the room.

I joined Etaa by the fire, noting how she drew away as I sat down, and asked if she had understood us.

Her eyes met mine briefly, and wounded me with their misery, before she signed, —He would hurt me. He fears the blessings of the Mother.

I nodded, reminding her that here her "blessings" were sins, but assuring her that she would not be hurt while she was under my protection. —Tell me, Etaa, what did you think of the archbishop? He's the high priest of my people.

—He does not like you.

It surprised a laugh out of me.

—And he is a poor man to be priest, who cannot feel another creature's soul. To deny the second sight is to deny one's—gods.

—But the Gods say they wish it that way.

—Then they are false gods, who do not love you.

Then they are false Gods. . . . I watched the flames eat darkness for a long moment. —But they're here, Etaa, and powerful; and so is their Church. The archbishop would gladly see you burn as a witch, and so would almost anyone. But I believe as you do, that hearing is a blessing—and I want to share it. You will give my children the "second sight." And you can give it to me.

—From now on, if you hear anyone come into my presence you will tell me immediately, wherever we are. It's not an easy thing to be king in these times, or any times. I need your help . . . and you need mine. If anything should happen to me, there's no one who would protect you. You'd be burned alive, and suffer terrible agony, and your soul would be lost to your Goddess forever. Do you understand me? I knew that she had understood everything, from the changes that crossed her face. Slowly she nodded, her hands pressing the stiff, gold-embroidered russet that covered her stomach.

Unthinking, and somehow ashamed, I reached out in a gesture of comfort, only to have her wither under my touch like a blossom in the frost. Gently I went on touching her, but to no avail, and when at last I took her to the bedchamber, she lay as limp and deathly unresponsive as ever. As she turned her face from a final kiss I caught her shoulders and shook her, saying, "Damn you, you heathen bitch!" I let her fall back against the pillows, remembering that she didn't understand me, and raised my hands into the lamplight. She lifted her own defensively, as though she thought I was going to strike her, and I brushed them aside. —Watch me! Do you think a man enjoys taking a corpse to bed? I know what you are with your own people; why should you turn away from me? I'll have an heir from you whatever you do; you're mine now, so why not enjoy it—

Her fist flew out and struck me across the jaw. I jerked back in painful disbelief, while her hands leaped in hysterical fury.

—I serve my Goddess in holiness, I am not a Neaane whore! You have stolen a priestess, you have defiled Her, murderer, and She will never give you heirs. Neaa, you murdered my husband, whom I loved. Soul-stealer, I would burn a thousand times and weep forever in the wind before I would give you pleasure! Never will I . . . never . . . Hywel . . . She crumpled into sobbing and meaningless gestures, and buried her face in the cover.

Slowly I rose from the bed, and groping for my lenses, forgave the only woman who had ever struck a king of Tramaine.

I still took her to my bed as often as I could, although her wretchedness had driven all the pleasure from it; for, priestess of fertility though she might be, and king though I might be, children are a rare gift of fortune since the plague. And the Gods have done nothing to change that. I was away from her much of the time after our arrival in Newham, though, being engrossed as usual in affairs of state. And so I could scarcely believe my eyes when fat old Mabis, whom I had sent to serve Etaa, informed me gleefully of seeing signs that I was going to be a father. She was my nurse as a child (and so accepted most of my quirks, including a godless mistress), and assured me that if anyone could tell, it was Mabis. Giddy with pride, I forgot the quarreling of my nobles and the complaints of the burghers; I left even my watchman behind and ran like a boy to find Etaa.

She sat as she so often did, gazing out the high windows, her hair hanging at her back in a heavy plait, for Mabis couldn't get her to wear a covering. She looked up in amazement as I entered; composing myself with an effort, I managed to keep from destroying the moment by lifting her up in my arms. She seemed to know why I had come, and I thought, relieved, that maybe traces of pride hid behind her dark eyes as I bent my knee before her. I gave her my heartfelt thanks and asked what gift I could give her, in return for the one she had given me.

She glanced out the open window for a moment, her face lit with rainbows from the colored glass; when she looked back, her hands were stiff with emotion. —Let me go outside.

—That's all you want?

She nodded.

—Then you shall have it. Carefully I took her hand, and ordering my watch to keep well behind, led her outside into the palace gardens. Etaa somehow belonged in the beauty of roses and pale marisettes, her own wild grace set free from the gray stone confines of the palace walls. I took her to the limit of the green slopes overlooking the placid Aton and the edge of Newham-town on the river's farther shore. I tried to describe for her the city that was the heart of Tramaine, the bright, swarming mass of humanity, the marketplaces, the pageantry of New Year's and the celebrations of Armageddon Day. She gazed and questioned with a hesitant wonder that pleased me, but I thought she seemed glad when the peaceful bowers closed her in again.

We made our way along drowsy, dappled paths heavy with the heat of a late summer's afternoon, and I found it hard to believe the sun was already half hidden as it sank behind Cyclops. And as we walked I saw the drawn, anguished look fade from Etaa's face for the first time since midsummer. At one point, we unexpectedly came upon young Lord Tolper and his sweetheart, in a compromising position on the grass. I took Etaa's arm and led her quickly away, before the blushing lord felt required to rise and make a bow; as we turned to go I saw a quick, sweet smile of remembrance touch her lips, and felt a pang of envy.

Because I had so little time to myself, I instructed Mabis to accompany Etaa in the future into the gardens—and to do anything else that might be required for her health and comfort. Mabis confided that she had already been gathering healthful herbs for the babe at Etaa's request; for, bless her pagan soul, the girl had the skill of ten Newham physicians, and had even told her of a poultice to ease the ache in an old woman's back. Mabis was deeply religious in her own way, but she had never liked the queen, and Etaa's thoughtless kindnesses and lack of vanity had won her heart.

Etaa had little contact with the court in the beginning, partly at my wish and partly at her own. Yet she found another friend in the palace before long, a fellow outcast of sorts: young Willem, who was one of my pages. He was a strange, nervous boy, his hair as flaxen as her own was black, who seemed to be constantly starting at unseen sights and sometimes even to see around corners. He stuttered in both noble and common speech, as though not only his lips but even his own fingers wouldn't obey him. One afternoon I came to call on Etaa in her chambers and found him sitting at her feet before the fire, their faces half in the green light of waning eclipse, half ruddy with fireglow. They looked up at me almost as one, and Willem scrambled to his feet to bow, barely concealing his dismay at the arrival of his king. I gathered that Etaa had been telling him a story, and asked her to continue, feeling that I would be glad of a little diversion too.

She took up her story again almost self-consciously, a Kedonny tale of how a wandering people had come to settle and find a home at last. I grew fascinated myself by the realism of it, even though it was riddled with allusions to the supernatural powers of the Mother. It struck me that this must be the story of how they had come to our borders, in the time of the second Barthelwydde king, nearly two hundred years before.

I was fascinated too by the motions of her hands, so quick and bold compared to the refined gestures of the court poets, whose graceful imported romances usually left me yawning. Occasionally she would stumble, breaking the trancelike rhythm of her tale, and I remembered that she had to translate as she told, a feat that would leave my poets ill with envy.

When her tale was finished I sent Willem away to his neglected duties, and, impulsively, asked Etaa if she would come with me to see our own collected lore. She nodded, politely curious. The child growing within her seemed to have given her a thing to love in place of the man she had lost; perhaps because of it—and because I no longer touched her—she tolerated me now, and sometimes almost seemed glad of my company.

I led the way into the part of the palace given over to the Gods; it was hung with gilt-framed paintings and ornate tapestries of religious scenes. I went there often, not for homage, but to visit the repository for the holy books. It had taken all the power and influence of the kingship to defy the clergy successfully, but I had been determined to study on my own those remnants of the Golden Age that the Gods deemed too complex—and possibly too heretical—for the layman. The priests who were entrusted with the books spent the greater part of their lives studying them, since they were presumably protected by their faith (or, I sometimes suspected, by their ignorance). I had had the best possible education, but even I found to my frustration that most of the learning from before the plague time was far above me. The Gods would give me no clues, of course, though they claimed omniscience, since they opposed my right to study the sacred lore. But then, they also refused to give guidance to the priests.

As we entered the corridors of the Gods a viridian-robed priest came to meet us, and I recognized him as Bishop Perrine, the archbishop's chief lackey. His bow was scarcely adequate, his lips moving in rigid formality. "Your majesty. You cannot possibly bring that—that woman here! It would be sacrilege to reveal the holy works to a—a pagan."

I smiled tolerantly, suspecting that after the morning's usual strife with the archbishop, this very scene had been secretly taking shape in my mind. "Bishop Perrine, this woman is acting as my watchman. I am quite sure she can't read—"

Etaa started, and I glanced past the bishop's shaven head to see one of the very Gods coming toward us down the hall. Bishop Perrine turned, following my gaze, and together we dropped down on one knee. Too late I noticed that Etaa still stood, defiantly facing the towering, inhumanly beautiful figure in robes lit with an unearthly inner glow. I signaled her to kneel but she ignored me, caught up in fearful amazement.

I waited while God regarded priestess in return, my knee grating on the unaccustomed hardness of the floor and my head thrown back until a crick began to form in my neck. At last an expression passed over his face that I almost took for appreciation; and remembering us, he gave us permission to rise, signing, —My pardon, your majesty, for causing you discomfort; but I forgot myself, at the sight of the opposition.

Bishop Perrine began apologies, his fingers knotting in nervous obsequiousness, but the God stopped him. —No need, Bishop Perrine—I understand. And she is charming, your majesty. I see why they say the Black Witch has enchanted you.

I inclined my head while I mastered a frown, and signed with proper deference. —She is no witch, Lord, but merely a handsome woman. Her beliefs are of no consequence; only primitive superstition.

—I am relieved to learn that. His hands expressed a faint mockery, each move slightly too perfect. —Etaa, can you deny the presence of the true Gods, now that you see one before you?

Slowly she nodded. —You are beautiful to see. But you are a man, and so you cannot be a god. There are no gods other than our Mother. Her face was serene, her eyes shone with belief. I had often envied unshakable faith, but never more than now.

Bishop Perrine shuddered visibly beside me and clutched his god-sign, but I saw the God laugh. —Well signed, priestess. Your belief may be misguided, but not even I can deny its purity. Bishop Perrine, I take it you sought to keep this woman from entering here. I commend you—but I think you should let her pass. Perhaps some further exposure to our beliefs would do her soul good.

Bishop Perrine dropped to the floor, and I sank grudgingly down beside him as the God passed. And as I led Etaa on to the repository, I wondered that a God should have treated us so affably. I knew that the various Gods who called on us had different manners, just as they had different faces when you were used to their splendor. But they were seldom so kindly disposed toward heretics, or anything that threatened the stability of their Church.

Etaa brushed the blue velvet of my sleeve. —Meron— She seldom called me by name, although it pleased me. —How is it that you do not believe in your own gods, when you've seen them all your life? Her hands moved discreetly, half hidden by her wide fur-trimmed sleeves.

I remembered my comment to her in the carriage, so long ago. —You don't believe in them because you say they look like men. Our scriptures tell us that they *are* like men; but I've seen them when they were not. I told her what I'd seen as a child. —So whatever they are, they're *not* the Gods of the scriptures who abandoned us long ago. But they control the lives of my people, and the peoples of all the adjoining lands, through the Church: these—false Gods.

She frowned. —It was only after the gods came that your people began to hate us. Are they cruel, then, to make your people cruel? Her eyes stole glances at the dark scenes displayed along the walls.

I shook my head. —No . . . they're not cruel to us. But they don't condemn cruelty toward non-believers. They want no competition, I think. I looked away from a woven witch-burning. —They've done good, useful things for us—driven the wild kharks from the countryside, helped us grow better crops, shown us how to control the shaking fever . . . they've made us—comfortable. Too comfortable, I sometimes think. As though . . . as though they wanted us to stay here forever, and be content never to regain the Golden Age again. And there *was* a Golden Age, I've seen proof of it, in the volumes we go to see now.

—Volumes? Books? Excitement lit her face. —We have a book in our village, that I've studied with the elders; it's said to be from the Blessed Time, when all people knew the touch of the Mother.

—You have that legend too? I stopped moving. —Then it must have been widespread—perhaps the whole world! Think of it, Etaa! But what knowledge we have left, the Gods keep hidden from anyone who could use it. My bitterness made my hands tighten. —The Church teaches us "humility" —not to strive, not to tempt fate, or the Gods, but follow the old worn path to sure salvation. It teaches the people to hate the "second sight" that could give them such freedom, and to hate your people most of all, because you make a religion of it. The Gods make us comfortable, but not because they love us. Damn th—

Etaa caught my hands suddenly, in a graceful grip that was like a vise; she forced them to her lips in a seemingly effortless kiss. I stared at her, astounded, and caught movement in the mirror at the side of my lenses. Down the hall, the archbishop stood watching us intently; she had kept me from cursing the Gods in his presence. I let her know by my tightened hands that I understood. She freed me, and I signed, —Come, love, first go with me to see the holy relics. We continued to the repository; the archbishop did not follow us. I wondered if he had seen enough.

I thanked Etaa, and for a moment she touched my hands again; but then she only looked away, signing stiffly, —Your life is my life, and my child's, as you have said. You need not thank me for that.

But I felt she had been repaid when her hands rose in wonder as we entered the repository and she saw the books—thirty-five volumes resting on yellow satin, above the elaborately embellished study table. Two priests were at their contemplation; not having attendants with me, I went myself and tapped them on the shoulder, asking them to leave. Their faces flashed surprise, acceptance—and a hint of scandal as they passed Etaa and left us alone. Etaa went to stand by the sloping desk, looking down reverently on the smooth, timeless pages of the open books. And then I learned one more thing about the barbaric Kedonny—that their priestess read the printed words of the old language as well as any man of our own priesthood.

And so, though I had taken her with me originally out of a certain obstreperous pride, and because I valued her as a watchman, I began taking her with me for her opinions as well. Word of the pagan woman studying the holy books got rapidly back to the archbishop, and when he came to make his complaint I was forced to remind him sharply that he spoke to his king. I think despite his hunger for personal power he believed in the Church's tenets and its Gods, and was torn by the dilemma they created for him: he believed I committed sacrilege, but because a God had approved it there was nothing he could do to stop me. Or so I thought, even though I knew well enough he would do anything to get at the kingship, for the aspirations of his family and the furtherance of Church power.

As the dark noons of autumn passed into the bright, snowblind days of true winter, I continued to take Etaa with me to study the books, and to have her beside me as my watchman and companion whenever the occasion allowed. Her coming motherhood grew obvious to all, and was the target for much discreet levity, and also more serious speculation. Also for some unpleasant and ugly rumors revolving on witchcraft, whose sources I thought I knew. I didn't bother to deal with them, however, being more concerned with other matters; particularly with the rebellious Kedonny, who stubbornly harried our borderlands even though the snows lay heavy on the earth. There were rumors that a new leader had emerged, using the defiling of a priestess to rally them, and so I sent messengers to my most trusted border lords, telling them to be on guard. But the Kedonny would strike whenever a back was turned, and then fade away into the hills, and their Mother shielded them in Her snowy cloak, as Etaa would have signed—if she'd known. My best leaders seemed helpless against the determined fanaticism of the Kedonny chief, a man called only "the Smith," who was becoming a bogeyman in Tramaine fit to compete with the Godseye that looked down on my people's sinful lives.

At last came Midwinter's Day—a day I would not have marked except that I found Etaa kneeling awkwardly at her hearth, wearing dappled green velvet. She was tossing stalks of ripened wheat into the fierce blaze and reciting a ceremony of the Mother. Pale Willem crouched watching as if hypnotized, while his spotted pup chewed unnoticed at the tail of his jerkin. Mabis sat spinning in the far corner of the chamber, her round chill-reddened face set in righteous disapproval. I was mildly disturbed to see Willem so caught up in Kedonny ways; but his friendship with Etaa cheered them both, and lately I found it hard not to prefer Etaa to our own dour ways myself. But I chided Willem, and he disappeared, ghostlike as always, when I took Etaa away to visit the holy books.

That day she sat beside me as usual, though lately she found it hard to bend forward at the ornate table's edge. (Mabis had said my son—for I was sure it would be a son, just as I was sure he would hear like his mother—must be a strapping babe, perhaps even twins.) Her ungainly roundness charmed me even more than her former grace.

I had taken my lenses off in order to read close up, for with Etaa there, I had no fear of being caught unawares. She glanced down as I set the lenses on the table, and then suddenly she caught at my arm. —Meron, look— She picked up the end of the thin, dark strip that lay pinned under them, curling it between her fingers. —What is this? It's like glass, but soft as paper. And look—look! Tiny words, under your lens—

I squinted, unable to make them out, and reached for a magnifying glass. —It's plastic, that the Gods use . . . and that we used, once, in the Golden Age. A strange excitement filled me as Etaa pulled the rest of the tape out from under the shelf into the lamplight. —How did it get here? Could the Gods have forgotten—

Etaa took up the glass and held it over the plastic strip.

—Can you read it?

She didn't see me, but sat frowning, breathless with concentration, her hand toying with the silver bell at her ear. At last she looked up, her fingers barely moving as she signed, —I can read it. It is part of a book in the old language. . . . But it's from *before* the plague time.

—Are you sure? All our holy books had been written after the plague; though they mentioned the wonders of the Golden Age, they were clouded with the despair of a failing people, and many references were unclear. My hands shook. —Read it to me.

I held the glass and Etaa translated, until her eyes were red and her hands trembled with fatigue. And though many things were still unclear, because they were so far above us, one undeniable truth stood out: —All men *could* hear, in the Golden Age. I was right! Men weren't meant to be less than the Gods—men *were* Gods. The Church has lost the truth in fear since the plague time, and these false "Gods" use our superstition to control us. I took Etaa's weary hands and kissed them. —But our son will be the beginning of a new Golden Age, he'll hear and see clearly, and show my people the truth. He will be our greatest king. Etta smiled, caught up in my dreams, and if she smiled for her son and not for me, it didn't lessen the fullness of my joy.

And then the moment was torn by a lash of pain that raked my back, a blow that knocked me from my seat. My useless eyes met billows of indigo as I rolled, and a streak of light arcing down at my face; desperately I threw up my hands. But before the blade could find me again, a sweep of green velvet blocked my sight as Etaa flung herself on the attacking priest. Fair hands dimmed the shining blade, and somehow she drove him back from me while I got to my feet. I caught up my lenses and drew my dagger, only to see him fling her against the wall and bolt toward the door. I brought the priest down as he tried to get past me; his skull cracked against the flags, and the knife flew from his grasp.

And beyond him I saw Etaa curled on her side on the floor, racked with a spasm of pain. She pressed her stomach, staining the velvet with blood from her slashed hands. I looked down again into the face of my attacker, full of terror now as my dagger rested on his throat. And saw that he was no priest: dirty hair slipped from under his cap, his face was young, but grimy and pinched with hardship. He was a paid assassin out of the Newham stews, and I was sure he was a hearer as well. And I couldn't touch him—or his master—for the Church claimed jurisdiction here. My hand tightened on the dagger hilt, and I would have slit his throat. But as blood traced my blade across his neck I felt Etaa's eyes on me, and I sickened. "Let the archbishop try you, then, for your failure, 'priest,' " I said. "And I pity you—" I struck him on the head with the dagger's butt, and felt him go limp.

Then I went to Etaa and fell on my knees beside her, raising her head. Her eyes sought me almost with hunger, and for a moment they filled with wild joy as her wounded hands brushed my face. But they tightened into fists with another spasm as she tried to form signs. —Meron . . . my child. My child . . . comes—

My throat tightened with despair. It was sacrcely half the year since her conception, and that was too soon, too soon . . . I felt the back of my tunic soaking with blood, but the assassin's knife had caught in the folds of my cape and the wound was not deep. I picked Etaa up in my arms, gasping with pain, and started back through the endless halls.

Halls that were endlessly empty, until suddenly I came on the archbishop and Bishop Perrine. The archbishop saw us first, and laughter fell from his face, leaving blank horror. He hurried toward me, arms outstretched, until he met my eyes; then, and only then, did I ever see my cousin afraid. He stopped. "Your majesty—" His lips quivered; Bishop Perrine's eyes went to the trail of red on the stones behind us, and he dropped to his knees, babbling incoherently.

"My Lord . . . bishop." I staggered against the wall to save my precious burden. "If my son dies, my lord, not even the Gods will find sanctuary from me." I pushed grimly past him, and saw in my mirror that he was hurrying on toward the repository.

I found a guardsman and friendly halls at last, and summoned aid. My physicians swarmed around me like flies, binding my wound and begging me to rest; but I stood at the door of the chamber where they had taken Etaa, until finally my knees buckled and I could not stand. And then I remember little except my helpless fury, at events and my own weakness, until I woke in my canopied bed, hemmed in by kneeling attendants, to face a God. I struggled toward the only thing of real importance: —Etaa . . . my child—?

I thought the God smiled, though I couldn't focus. —I have been with them—

"No!" I lunged at him, and was pulled back by my horrified attendants.

They gibbered apologies, but he waved them aside. —The lady is well, and asks for you. And your son—yes, your majesty, you son—will live. He is well grown for one born so early, and we will watch over him.

I sank back into the pillows. —Forgive me, lord, I—I was not myself. I thank you. And now, doctor, with your aid I would go to see my Etaa . . . and my son.

The Church proclaimed that my assailant was a mad priest, who had wrongly believed me guilty of sacrilege concerning the Church's holy books; he had been summarily excommunicated and put to death for his treason, upon order of the archbishop. There were mutterings in the Church faction at court that the priest was hardly mad, but in the celebration at the birth of a royal heir they were scarcely heard. I named my son Alfilere, after my father, and to me he was the most beautiful sight on Earth. And second only to him was his mother, her own face shining with pleasure as she gazed down upon him in his golden cradle or caressed him with bandaged hands.

I began to take her with me everywhere now, seeking her impressions of the things she saw at court; and though she protested, I seated her openly beside me at table. The queen still sat at my other hand, unwilling to give up any of her position, though her eyes drove daggers into my back. Her brother absented himself from the great hall these days, and I wondered if he was sharpening a new blade of his own. But he would never dare such a blatant attack on me again, and though my advisers knew of his treason and urged me to act against him, I refused. If I attacked my cousin I would risk civil war, and I would not bring that on my people for the sake of personal revenge. But I no longer went anywhere without attendants, and I saw that my guard kept watch at all times over Etaa and her child.

But though tension whispered in the halls like the chill drafts of winter, it could not discourage the spring that brightened my heart at the thought of my newborn son, or the nearness of Etaa. For the Armageddon Day festivities, I taught her, amid much laughter, to dance. I had always hated memorizing intricate patterns and steps, the watching of ceiling mirrors, the need to be constantly keeping count. But she was enchanted at this new challenge to her imagination, and her enthusiasm caught me up and made me feel the beauty of the dance.

The Armageddon celebrations, mirrored in Etaa's delighted eyes, had not seemed so bright since I was a boy, and as I carried my son in my arms I imagined how the same wonders would delight him too: the poets and jugglers and acrobats, the trained hounds and morts, the magicians flashing colored fire, even the Gods who presided, resplendent in their shining auras. All the gaudily clad folk feasting and dancing, driving away the cold bleakness of dark noons that marked the equinox and the grating end of a cruel winter beyond the walls.

I think, looking back, that I had never been happier than on that evening, when Etaa danced beside me. Gowned in the fragile colors of spring, her shining hair bound with pearls, she was the very goddess of the Earth. Her cheeks were flushed with excitement and her dark eyes radiant; after the last dance I took her in my arms and kissed her, and she did not pull away. Anything seemed possible to me then, even that someday she might come to love me . . . as I had come to love her, this captive goddess, in a way that I had never loved any woman.

But, as I have always known in my saner moments, not all things are possible, even for kings. And not long afterward Etaa turned cold eyes on me as I entered her chamber, looking up over Alfilere's dark curly head as he fed at her breast.

I hesitated. —Etaa, is something wrong?

Mabis got up heavily from her stool. She moved to sit facing away from us, still knitting, her ruddy face showing trouble and concern.

Etaa did not answer me for a moment, but rose and took Alfilere to his cradle near the fire, where she stood smiling and rocking him gently. She had refused a new nurse, preferring to feed and care for her own babe, another virtue which had pleased old Mabis. And indeed, my son's mother was better than any nurse, for she could "feel" his needs; she grew uneasy if he was ever beyond her hearing. At last she came back to me, the smile fading again, and I repeated my question.

Her pink-scarred hands snapped up with accusation. —Meron, I know the truth now, about my people. That they're making war on Tramaine, and being killed, because you've stolen me. I know that they demand my return—and beyond that, only to be left in peace by your witch-burners. But instead you send them soldiers, to kill and burn all the more. And you have kept it from me! And made me . . . made me forget . . . A strange emotion tormented her face, her hands twitched into stillness.

—Where did you learn this, Etaa?

She shook her head.

—Willem—

—You will not hurt him! Anger and fear knotted her fingers.

—I would not hurt a child for repeating gossip.

—But it's true?

—Yes.

Her fingers searched the rough edge of the tapestry that swayed in the draft along the wall. —Then let me go home to my people.

I looked away, feeling disappointment stab me like an assassin's blade. —I . . . I cannot do that. You wouldn't leave your child. And I will not give up my son. Are you so unhappy here? Can't you tell your people you're content to stay? I'll make peace with them, pay whatever restitution . . . I—need you, Etaa. I need you here with me. I depend on you now, I—

She shut her eyes. —Meron. The man who leads my people, who demands me back, the man you call "the Smith": he is my husband.

—Your husband is dead!

—No! Her foot stamped the floor.

—You saw him yourself, broken on the rocks! No man could survive that. He was a coward; he killed himself, he abandoned you to me, and I won't let you go. I drew a breath, struggling for control. —Your people raid and slaughter mine, and take their heads. You damn *our* souls—by our beliefs dismembered spirits cannot be freed by cremation. If there's war, then the Kedonny bring it on themselves!

Etaa drew herself up stiffly. —If you won't release me, he will come and take me!

I frowned. —If he can rise from the dead, then perhaps he will. But I doubt if even you can expect that of the Mother.

She crossed her arms, her eyes burning.

I left the chamber.

She stayed in her rooms from then on, refusing to accompany me anywhere, the drawn look of grief she had first worn returning to her face. When I came to see my son she would sit by the fire and turn her back on me, wordless. Once I came and sat beside her on the cushioned bench, with Alfilere squirming bright-eyed on my knees, wrapped in a fur bunting. I clapped my hands and saw him laugh, and as I offered him ringed fingers to chew on, looked up to see Etaa smile. I took back my fingers and signed, —Who could ask for a handsomer son? But he doesn't favor his father, I fear, little dark-eyes— I smiled hopefully, but she only looked away, brushing the silver bell at her ear, and tears showed suddenly on her cheeks.

Angry with Willem, at first I had forbidden him to visit her again; but I'd relented, knowing her solitude and sorrow. Not long after, I found him with her, his pale head in her lap, his thin shoulders shaken with sobs. She looked up as I came toward them, her eyes filled with shared pain; but Willem did not, and so she lifted his head from her lavender skirts. He rose unsteadily to make a bow, then sank exhausted onto the wine-red cushions beside her, wiping his face on his sleeve.

But I stood frozen in my place, because I had seen the thin tracks of drying blood that ran down his neck and jaw. Suddenly all his strange, frightened prescience fitted into place, and I realized the truth: my own page was a hearer, and somehow until now his family had managed to keep it a secret. Until now. My stomach twisted: his ears had been put out by the Church.

As though she had followed my thoughts, Etaa signed bitterly, —It was your Archbishop Shappistre. He hounded Willem for being with me, until he learned that Willem felt the Mother's touch—and see what he's done! He persecutes all who have Her blessings, he almost killed my child—he almost killed you! Your own kinsman! How can you let him go free, if you are king; why don't you challenge him?

I reached to the crooked scar along my back, caught in my own bitter outrage. The archbishop's open attempt to destroy me had failed, and now he waged a subtler war, spreading rumors, subverting those I trusted, tormenting those I loved. I had the power to strike him down, even in the face of the Gods; but I could not. —Etaa, it's not that simple. This isn't some villager's dispute, I can't take him out on the mead and thrash him! The royal line is split in two, and with it the loyalties of the nation; I rule a land at peace because I have tried to keep them reconciled. The archbishop is my counterbalance, but he'd upset the scales if he could, with his dreams of a Church-ruled state. He would throw this country into civil war to achieve it; he cares nothing for consequences. If I charged him with treason I'd do the same. He will stop at nothing; but I stop a long way before that.

Etaa stroked Willem's drooping head. –I don't understand the needs of nations, Meron . . . and you don't understand the needs of women and men. Suddenly she looked up at me, her face anguished. –He'll destroy you, Meron! Don't let him, don't . . . Her hands dropped hopelessly into her lap; she rose and turned away, going to the baby's cradle to comfort her gentle son.

Two days later, Willem was gone. The other pages said he had run away home. But one of Etaa's earrings, the tiny silver bells that she always wore, was missing too. I asked her where it was, and too carelessly she signed that she had lost it. And so I knew that Willem had gone east to find the Smith.

Slowly, with all the pain of birth, winter gave way at last to spring, while the Kedonny raided on our borders. Etaa mourned in her chambers, and the New Year's revels on the green were a bright, shallow mockery of the past.

And while I slept that night and dreamed of happier times, Etaa and my son disappeared.

Frantic with loss, I had the countryside searched and searched again, but there was no sign of them. There was no rumor, no clue; it was almost as if they had never been. I could get no rest, and my own lords said openly that I looked like a man possessed. The archbishop, smiling, said that perhaps the Earth had swallowed them up–and I almost came to believe him. But I learned my coachman had disappeared on the same night as Etaa, and some said they thought my carriage had gone in the night, and come back carrying no one. And so I wondered if the truth lay not in the Earth but in the sky . . . and the Gods had taken their revenge on me.

But the Kedonny ate deeper into my lands, and finally I was forced to abandon my search. I planned to raise a full army and put them to rout; but as I sent out calls to gather men, I discovered how well my archbishop had done his ungodly work. His rumors of my bewitchment had taken hold: my own people believed the Black Witch had snared me in a spell and addled my mind, then disappeared like the accursed thing she was, stealing even my son to be put to some terrible blasphemous use. They believed I would betray them to the Kedonny in battle, and that the Gods themselves had abandoned me.

Even lords who were always loyal to my father's line have deserted me for the archbishop, and those who still support me get little support themselves for the raising of an army. The word is abroad in the land that it is suicide to ride with me to war—that if I am denied, and destroyed, then the forces of Right will be served, and the Gods will save them from the pagan hordes. Damn the Church! The Gods have never intervened in a war of men; I doubt they'll do it now.

And so I leave today, with what forces I can gather, to go and save my kingdom myself, if I can. Perhaps then this new storm of ignorance will pass, and not inundate us all. Perhaps. Or perhaps it is already too late. . . .

If so, then maybe it is best that Etaa has gone, and taken my son. I only pray, to whatever true

Gods may be, that they are safe, and that some day her son will return to claim his throne, and be the greatest of our kings. If she chose to leave me, I cannot blame her, for I never had the right to take her as I did. But I loved her, and I pray she will remember that too, and forgive me a little.

I often wonder if she ever loved me. If so, it was more than I deserved. But sometimes there was a look, or a sign —The hands of the summer wind are as warm and light as your touch, Etaa; it may be that your Mother has stolen you home after all. Watch over my son, and forgive his father. Give him your blessings, as you gave them to me. Etaa . . . I think I will not see you again.

But come, my lords; the Godseye keeps watch on us, and the sun is already high. They say a smith may look at a king: then let it be the last thing he ever sees!

Part 3: The God

I understand that I'm speaking today because you wondered how a "naïve kid" in the Colonial Service was inspired to solve the Human Problem. The answer is simple—I loved Etaa, and Etaa was the mother of Alfilere.

You probably all remember the situation at the time. The Colonial Service had come upon the Humans not long before: an intelligent life form based on carbon rather than silicon, but oxygen-breathers and compatible with roughly the same temperature range that we are. That made them another competitor, but only marginally; and if they were anything else but Humans, we could have expected to coexist with them. But our studies of their ongoing culture, and the scanty records of their past, indicated they were the most unrelentingly and irrationally aggressive species we'd ever encountered. Combined with a high technology, it would have made them the most dangerous, too. We'd live in peace with them willingly enough, under the circumstances, but the question I'd always heard was whether *they* would live in peace with *us*. The majority Conservative opinion was that it wasn't likely, and so our sector council ordered us to intervene, and stall their cultural progress. The Liberal faction in the Service objected, doing their best to prod the Human status quo, and that was how the trouble started.

I'm a xenobiologist, and at the time I was just beginning my career; I was also too inexperienced to question policy then, and so I blindly supported the majority's stand on Humans. Especially since I'd had to live among Humans, to study (and watch) them, as the "coachman" for the God-hating king of Tramaine. When the Libs gave restricted records to the king, and then openly incited the neighboring Kotaane to war, we Conservatives retaliated by kidnapping Etaa, the king's Kotaane mistress, and her son, his heir. I was chosen to do the actual deed, because of my strategic position—and, frankly, my naïveté. All I had to do was keep the pair safely out of the way, they told me, and at the same time I could experience my first change-study of an unknown world. . . . All I had to do was spend an eternity alone, I discovered, on a desolate abandoned world with no one for company but a superstitious alien woman and a squalling alien brat. I didn't know whether to be honored by the responsibility, or ashamed of being used. But I did my duty, and stole her away to the outer moon.

I sent Etaa drugged wine, and shuttered all the ports; she never knew what had happened, even when I brought the shuttle down near the ruins of the dead colony and opened the lock. I watched her on the screens as she stepped outside, waiting while the first rush of stunned dismay took her. She stumbled back, clutching her child protectively against her as the cold wind gusted, swirling the drab rust-brown grit into stinging clouds. Beyond us the naked, stony slope swept upward toward the ruins of the Human town, fangs of bitterness snapping at the clouds. I'd seen it once before, but never like this, knowing I couldn't leave it. My own eyes burned with the bleakness and the memory of the stinging wind. It would be hard to learn the unity of this world . . . it was easy to see why the Humans had failed to.

I don't know what thoughts were in Etaa's mind then; only that they probably weren't the ones I expected. But confusion and despair were on her face as she started down the ramp, the wind tugging at her long cape and stiff, ungainly skirts. Her baby had begun to cry, wailing with the wind. For the first time she was real for me, touching my emotions and stirring—pity. This was the stolen woman, used by a ruthless king, whose misery I seemed to be tied to from the start, when I'd piloted the king's carriage in her capture. She was only another victim of the cruel and senseless schisms that divided these wretched Humans, and she'd suffer more now and never understand why, because of them, and because of us. . . . I felt unease pull down pity: Did I have the right—? But she'd been a pawn, she would be a pawn; maybe that was her destiny, and this was mine.

I left the controls at last, bracing myself to deliver the final horror to her. I'd gotten rid of my Human makeup, and knew my form would be starting to slip after the stress of the flight. And no Human had ever seen a "God" unmasked, even a God who passed for a coachman. Avoiding the velvet cushions on the floor, I went to stand at the lock.

—Meron—? She turned with a gasp to stare up at me, her hands asking the question. I remembered she was a Kotaane priestess, and could hear; the speculation was that the king had taken her precisely because she *could,* out of his hatred for tradition. Her eyes had brightened with hope and something more as she turned. It froze into terror as she saw me, and she backed away, her fingers stiffening out in a sign to ward off evil. It was too much like an obscenity popular with the king's retainers; I almost laughed. That would have been the final cruelty. I caught it in time and only spread my hands in a peace gesture. I signed, —I will not harm you, Lady Etaa. Have no fear. She shook her head, keeping her distance. I wondered what I must look like to her—a mockery of a Human made of bread dough, or clay. I ducked back into the king's "carriage" to get my hooded jacket, thinking the more I covered the better. But as I disappeared I heard her startled cry and footsteps behind me on the ramp. She appeared at the lock in a swirl of dust, and dropped to her knees at my feet. —Oh, please, don't leave me here! The baby whimpered as her signing jostled him, inside her cape. I stared down at her, stunned; but seeing my face again she faltered, as if she saw her own doom instead. Looking away, she placed her wriggling child tenderly on a red velvet cushion, then forced her eyes back to mine, signing, —Then have mercy on my child. Take him with you, he's no harm to anyone! He is a prince, return him to—to his father, King Meron. You'll be rewarded! Give him to anyone . . . but let him live—

I bent down and picked up the child; he gazed at me in fascination, and suddenly he began to laugh. Inexplicably delighted, I held him close; then, slowly, I passed him back to his mother's arms. Hope shattered on her face, and she flinched when I touched her.

I stepped back. —Etaa, you aren't being abandoned in this godforsaken place. I am your guardian; I'll stay with you here, to look after you and your child. You've been . . . exiled, and it will be a hard life for us both. But it won't last forever, only until—certain matters are settled in Tramaine. But it has to be this way until then; you have no choice. This is your new home.

She watched rigidly, the need to ask a hundred questions struggling against the certainty that she didn't need to ask, but only accept, and endure, this new trial. She looked down at last, and I saw the trembling lines of her face grow quiet with resolve; she would adapt. I felt relieved, and somehow surprised.

—Who has ordered this? Not . . . not the king? Her dark eyes flickered up again with a kind of urgency.

—No. I reassurred her, thinking how she must hate the man, and not wanting the truth to seem any harsher than it was. —It—is the will of the Gods, Etaa.

Her flush of relief turned to a sudden frown,

and she looked hard at me for a moment. But she pulled back into her silence, and signed nothing more, waiting for me.

I gave her a clingsuit and boots like my own to replace her awkward gown, then waited outside the craft in the wind, knowing the preoccupation with bodily shame that these heterosexuals had. She appeared at last, with her hair bound up and her child slung at her back in the folds of her cape. The heavy jacket flapped around her like a tent, but I could see that the suit had adapted to her well enough to keep her warm. I sealed the clasps on her jacket while she watched me, intent and suspicious. Then I unloaded supplies, and sealed the hatch behind us. The lifeboat rose silently; the king's carriage would be home before he missed it. I wished we could have been, too.

We struggled up the hill toward the ruined town, battered by blowing grit and dead, unidentifiable vegetation. The ragged maze of the tree-eaten ruins broke the back of the wind as we reached the summit; we stood panting and rubbing our burning eyes while the wind moaned and clattered in frustration overhead. I led Etaa through the rubble to a shelter that stood intact, a prefabricated box that still had its roof. As we stumbled along the street she watched with awe, but without the sickly dread Tramanians had for the cities of their dead past. I wondered if she had ever seen a pre-plague Human city even on her own world, not knowing she didn't understand that this wasn't her own world.

The Humans had colonized the inner, major moon of a gas giant they had named Cyclops, which circled the yellow star Mehel. This outer, barely smaller moon was just marginally habitable, and they had only tried to establish a colony here to escape from the disease that decimated them at home. They had failed, and all that remained was this town, under skies that were endlessly gray with clouds. Etaa never saw the change in the heavens, and never knew there had been one because she never asked a question: we communicated as little as possible, and often I caught her staring at me, her eyes somewhere between fear and speculation.

But once she insisted that she needed to gather healthful herbs for the baby, and when I tried to tell her that our supplies had everything she would need, she gathered him up protectively inside her jacket and slipped out the door. I went after her, armed, because I still wasn't sure exactly what else was making its home in this dead city. For over an hour I watched her search for a trace of the life she knew, but nothing had survived the departure of the Humans. At last, shivering and defeated, she brushed past me without meeting my eyes, and returned to the shelter. After that she communicated less than ever, only glaring at me as if this terrible strangeness were somehow my doing too. She never ventured outside again by choice, and never left her son alone with me.

I spent most of my time outside, struggling with equipment in the bitter wind as I tried to gather background data for my ecological change-study. The deserted Human town crouched like a tethered beast on the rim of the plateau, waiting with un-Human patience for the return of its masters while time and the gnarled hands of the tree-shrubs worried it toward oblivion. Beyond the plateau's rim eons of sediment from some murky forgotten sea lapped away to grim distant peaks. But closer in, the stone had been shattered by countless faultings, eroded by the winter rains and the sand-sweeping wind until a network of twisting sheer-walled canyons had been eaten into its undulating plain. The eternal wind sang through the maze, whipping the iron-reddened dust of the washes, where flashing water roared and passed with every drowning downpour. The wind was a bully, tumbling the slow, heavy clouds, breaking them open for a sudden glimpse of burnished heaven and shutting them again before you found it. Land and sky merged at the dusky horizon, and everywhere the colors repeated, shadow-violet and rust, burnt orange and fragile lavender, all merging toward gray in the somber light.

What flora there was was carbon-based, mainly lichen and an omnipresent hummocky dark moss. The sparse scatter of higher forms climaxed in the tree-shrub that dotted the ruins, a grotesque thing that looked like it was growing upside down. I knew almost nothing about the animal life, the preliminary survey having been so cursory; from time to time dark things scuttled at the edge of my vision, and in the updrafts above the canyons I could sometimes glimpse a shadowy, undulating form. As I began to watch these "gliders" in flight, I first felt the change stir within me, a blind groping toward understanding, a restlessness, a formless need to seek the new equilibrium . . . for the first time I wasn't being forced into a preset mold, this time my body would find its own place freely in the unity of a new unknown. I was fulfilled in the knowledge that now I knew nothing of the life on this world . . . but soon, in a way, I would know everything.

And I wondered whether that was the true reason why we feared the Humans: for all the studies we'd done, we had never been to their origin place or really "gone native" among them. Because we were forced to non-natural imitation among this transplanted stock, we had never really *felt* what it was to be Human. We wore false faces, false bodies; we saw them act and react around us, but never knew what moved them to it.

Exploring the dead Human town, I found myself thinking of how it would feel to colonize an unknown world, to think you were secure and settled—and then to be struck by an alien epidemic: to see half the population die, the survivors left genetically mutilated, sterile and deaf and blind . . . to lose contact with the rest of the Human kind, to see your proud civilization torn apart by fear and your technology crumble to barbarism . . . to lose everything.

And then to come back, to begin again from nothing in a treacherous, silent universe, and come so far—only to be stopped again, by us. They had adapted; and there was nothing we admired more. Yet the Colonial Service held them back; we counted ourselves lucky that they had suffered so much. And I'd never had any doubt about the morality of our position.

But then I shared a deserted world with Etaa, and passed through the change, and was changed in ways I had never meant to be.

The changes were resisted, in the beginning, as change always is. My physical deterioration of form had slowed, while my body chemistry fumbled toward an understanding of its new environment; but I stayed longer and longer out in the bitter days of the alien spring. My physical change was also slowed by the presence of Etaa; I went on instinctively mimicking the form of my closest companion—my only companion, for dreary weeks on end, until the return of Iyohangziglepi with supplies, and with them, the chance to hear a spoken word again and see a friendly face. And hear the gradually more agonizing reports that things in Tramaine continued unresolved. The Liberals had aroused the Kotaane, and now there seemed to be no stopping them. And as long as the uncertainty lasted, the king's son had to be securely out of it.

I began to worry sometimes that Etaa would break down in her endless solitude, since she rarely even had my escape into the greater world around the dead town. But she came from a people used to long, buried winters; and if she sometimes tended the fire below the window needlessly, or slept too long, and cried in her sleep, I tried to leave her alone. We all cope however we can, and she wouldn't have listened anyway. But I watched her with her child, as I watched the gliders by day wheeling over the maze, and again I felt an indefinable shifting in my soul.

Her thoughts were wrapped in her eternal cloak of silence, and only the baby, Alfilere, could draw her out. She would sit rocking him for hours while rain dinned on the roof, the silver bell she wore on one ear singing softly. She made him toys from scraps, smiled when he pulled her hair, tickled him while he played naked on her cloak by the fire, until their laughter filled the bleak room with light. She made the best of their new captivity, and so her son thought the world was a delightful place.

But sometimes as he fed at her breast her gaze would drift out of the present; a wistfulness would fill her eyes like tears and pass into a deeper knowledge that was wholly alien, and wholly Human. Sometimes too she would look into her child's face as though she saw someone else there, and then cover his face with longing kisses. She called him by a Kotaane name, "Hywel," and never "Alfilere," and I suspected that she knew he was her husband's child, and not the king's—this child of hope and sorrow. This child who was the center of her world—to whom Etaa, who was named "the blessed one," could never give the most unique and wonderful "blessing" she possessed, the gift of speech. Because she would never know she possessed it.

Her Alfilere was a bright, gentle baby who smiled more than he cried, and only cried when he had a reason. His awareness of the world grew every day, and soon I shared Etaa's fascination at each change. But when he first found his voice, babbling and squeaking to himself for hours on end, she only watched him with perplexity. Her people believed that hearing was the manifestation of another's thoughts and soul, and I knew this was her first child. Though she clapped her hands to get his attention, she never made another sound for him except her laughter, only moving her hands over and over while he watched, repeating the signs for simple words. Usually he would only catch her fingers and try to stuff them into his mouth.

And watching this woman, who was strong and fertile and gifted with full hearing and sight, who represented everything a Human could be . . . or should be . . . I suddenly realized what it would be never to find fulfillment, because you had even lost the sound of the word . . . the *feel*— In desperation I began to recite, "I am the eye that meets my gaze, I am the limb . . ."

Etaa started and stared at me; I'd never spoken before in front of her. Surprise and consternation pulled at her face; she looked back at her son, whose cheerful babbling must have made as much sense as mine, and then across the room at me again. On an impulse I repeated the lines, and she frowned. She picked up the baby and moved to the far corner, huddling inside her tentlike jacket on her ruined mattress . . . touching her throat. She coughed.

It wasn't long before I caught her mimicking the sounds her baby made. In a week or so more she had learned to hum for him. At first I was half guilty about what I had done; but gradually I convinced myself that it wouldn't come to anything. Though I wasn't even sure anymore that I'd done anything wrong.

And then the day came when the clouds parted. As I prowled the rim of the canyons, grateful for the slowly warming weather, brilliance suddenly opened up around me and all across the canyonlands a shower of golden sunlight was falling. For a moment I stood gaping at the incomprehensible glory until, glancing up, I saw the red "eye" and the banded green face of Cyclops peering back at me, filling a ragged piece of sky so bright it was almost black. I had taken off my braces to free my legs for change—running had gotten to be awkward and nearly ridiculous—but I ran back to the shelter and ducked in the open doorway. "Etaa, come and look!"

She stopped Alfilere in mid-whirl as she danced him around the room, and blinked at me, her smile fading. I realized I'd been shouting. I repeated it in sign language. —You can see the sky.

She followed me outside, and set Alfilere down to roll in the springy moss while she stood beside me, entranced by the sun-brindled, golden land and sky. I had almost forgotten the majesty of Cyclops wearing the sun for a crown, only a little diminished even from this outer moon. I remembered again that the sky the Humans took so much for granted was the most beautiful one I had ever seen. —Look, Etaa, can you see that dark spot against the face of Cyclops? That's your Earth.

She reddened as if I had insulted her. Only then did I realize that she had no idea we were on another world, and in my blind inexperience I had no idea of what that could really mean. —We traveled to Laa Merth, the moon you see from Earth, in the king's carriage; the Gods can make it travel between the worlds. You can see your Earth, up in the sky now instead; both these worlds are moons of—

She shut her eyes angrily, refusing me. —The Mother is the center of all things. *This* is the Earth! She folded her arms, then turned away toward the edge of the cliff, a small, stubborn figure plucked by the wind. She was still the Mother's priestess, and I suddenly realized that she was as true a believer as any Tramanian, and that her chthonic Goddess was just as tangible and real. As if by her will, the clouds closed over the last shining piece of the sky and rain splattered down, pocking the russet dust with spots the size of kiksuye buds.

Etaa turned back from the cliff's edge as the rain began, her eyes scanning for her child–and screamed. I jerked around, following her gaze, to see the shadow-form of a glider plummeting like dark death out of the clouds toward little Alfilere. She came running, her arms waving desperately. I pulled my stunner and fired, not knowing where a glider was vulnerable, but hoping the shock would divert its strike. I ran too, and saw the incredible, leathery balloon of the glider billow with the shock, heard myself shouting, "Here, here–damn you!" And heard the piercing shrill of outrage, saw the sky darken as the glider swerved to strike at me. Warty mottled skin flayed me, I staggered with the impact of its shapeless bulk. I heard my own scream then and the glider's moaning wail as a pincer beak closed over my arm, sank in, and snapped my body like a whip into the air. The glider shuddered at my weight, and hysterically I saw myself being crushed where it fell. . . . But then suddenly my arm was free, the air brightened–and I slammed back down onto the earth. The glider soared out over the canyon's rim, still keening.

I lay in the patch of blessed moss staring up into the rain, feeling as if a stake had been driven through me, pinning me to the ground. My torn arm throbbed with the beating of my heart, and I drew it up, strangely light, to see that the end was gone, bitten through. I studied the oozing stump where my hand had been, somehow unimpressed, and then let it drop back to my side.

But it didn't drop, for Etaa caught it in her own

hands, making small moans of horror while Alfilere wailed his fright against my leg.

"'S all right, 's all right . . ." I said stupidly, wondering what had happened to my voice, and why she didn't seem to understand me. I managed to sit up, shaking her off, and then stand. And then finally to realize that I didn't know what I was doing, before I fell to my knees again, weeping those damn sticky silicon-dioxide tears and cursing. But strong arms pulled me up again, and with Alfilere on one arm and me on the other, Etaa led her two weeping children home out of the rain.

I collapsed on my bedding, just wanting to lie in peace and sleep it through, but Etaa badgered me with frantic solicitude. —I'm a healer; let me help you, or you will die! The blood—

And I discovered that with a hand missing, there was no way I could explain. I frowned and pushed her away, and finally I held up my wounded arm and shook it at her; it had closed off immediately, and there was no more blood, nothing that needed to be done. She pulled back with a gasp of disbelief and looked at me again, her eyes asking the questions I couldn't answer. Then she brushed my cheek gently with her fingertips, and there was no revulsion in her touch. At last I let her bury me in warm covers and build up the fire, and then I slid down and down into darkness, through layers of troubled dreams.

I slept for two days, and when I woke my mind was clear and fully my own again, and I was starving. As if she knew, Etaa plied me with hot soup that I almost gulped down, though it probably would have poisoned me. I rejected it unhappily, unable to explain again. She looked down, hurt and guilty, as though I were rejecting her. I touched her face, in the gesture of comfort I'd seen Humans use, and signed, one-handed, —Can't . . . can't. Mine . . . cans— I waved at my own food supply, stacked by the Human supplies on the dusty shelves by the door. Her head came up, as if she should have known, and she left me. I looked at my wound and saw signs that the tissue was regenerating already. But it only made me realize the bigger problem: I'd been slowly reabsorbing all my limbs. Now that there was a need, and a reason, how could I communicate anything?

Etaa returned with an armful of cans and dropped them beside me on the floor. Then, kneeling, she held out the pad and stylus I'd been using for my sketches outside. I took them; she signed, beaming with inspiration, —Write for me.

I'd heard the king had taught her to read the archaic "holy books," but I hadn't believed it. I printed, clumsily, "Can you read this: 'My name is Etaa.' " I handed back the pad.

She smiled and signed, —My name is . . . She glanced up at me, puzzled. We used an arbitrary sign/symbol system based on the Human alphabet to record the Human hand-speech, and she had never seen her name written down at all. I pointed at her. She smiled again. —My name is . . . The middle fingers curled and straightened on her left hand, she held her right hand turned palm down, toward the earth. —Etaa. I am a priestess, I can read it.

I smiled too, in relief, and showed her how to pull open cans.

After I had eaten she brought Alfilere to me, half asleep, and gently sat him in my lap. I cradled him in the crook of my wounded arm; he settled happily, trying to nurse my jacket. Etaa laughed, and a feeling both strange and infinitely familiar came to me like spring, and left me breathless . . . and content.

—Thank you for saving my child. Etaa's dark eyes met mine directly, without loathing. —I was afraid of you, before, because of your strangeness. I think there was no need to be afraid. You have been . . . have been very kind. Again her eyes dropped, heavy with guilt. I thought of the king.

I printed laboriously, shamed by my own hidden prejudices, "So have you; though you had every right to be afraid, and hate me. Etaa, my strangeness will keep growing with time. But believe me that it will never harm you."

She nodded. —I believe that. . . . Can't you eat the food I make? It's better than those— Her wrist flicked with faint disdain at the emptied cans; I wondered if they looked as disgusting to her as the coarse Human meals did to me.

I hesitated before I wrote an answer. "I can't eat meat." I didn't add that I couldn't eat anything at all that wasn't on a silicon base like my own body.

—The Gods do many things strangely, besides changing their shape. Meron was wiser than he knew; you are false gods indeed to his people. She watched me coolly, almost smug in her conviction. I remembered hearing of her confrontation with another God, back in the dreary halls of the royal palace.

She was probably gratified by my stupefaction. I wrote, "How did you know?"

—The king knows. He saw a God once in an inhuman form; he knows you are not the ones promised to his people.

I frowned. So that was why the king scorned the Gods: he had discovered the truth. Suddenly his repressed anger and his ill-concealed hatred of the Church fell into perspective, and I realized there could have been more to the man than royal arrogance and consuming ambition. But that hardly mattered now. "Who does the king think we are?"

—He doesn't know . . . and neither do I. We only know your power over us, over our people. She studied me, and her dark-haired child blissfully asleep again in my lap. —Who *are* you . . . what are you? Why do you interfere in our lives?

"Because we're afraid of you, Etaa."

Her eyebrows rose as she read the answer, and her hands rose for more questions, but I shook my head.

She hesitated, and then her face settled into a resigned smile. She signed, —Why is it that you don't wear golden robes like the other Gods?

I laughed and wrote, "I'm a young God. We don't have all the privileges." Besides which, it was impossible for a biologist to make valid observations of any xenogroup while wearing golden robes.

She smiled again, the conspiratorial smile of one who was herself a Goddess incarnate. —What shall I name you?

"Name me Tam." I gave her my name-sign among Humans, since Wic'owoyake would have been unmanageable. I felt myself yawn, a trait I'd picked up from the Humans too, and reluctantly gave up Alfilere's sleeping form to my own need for sleep. He clung to me with his strong, tiny hands as his mother lifted him away, and I felt a rush of pleasure that he had taken to me so. I slept again, and had more dreams; dreams of change.

I don't know exactly when I decided to teach Etaa to speak. The desire arrived on a wave of exasperation, as it got to be more and more trouble to write out every word of every answer I made. My hand regenerated, but the change overtook it, and my other hand was getting too stiff and stubby to make signs or hold a stylus. Teaching Etaa speech meant going against the rules in a way I had never even considered before, interfering with Human society by adding a major cultural stimulus. But then, I thought, what was I doing here with her in the first place, and what were the Libs doing waging war back in Tramaine? I'd be guilty of Liberalism too, but I had to be able to communicate—and so I convinced myself that even if she could learn to speak, it would never come to anything among a people who were still mostly deaf.

And so while the final drenching storm of the rainy season battered the helpless land and rattled on the roof, I explained to Etaa how she knew there *was* rain on the roof, when other Humans didn't. I called her attention to the sounds her child made, and the ones I'd made—and the ones she had begun to make herself. I showed her the patterns they could weave, as her hands wove patterns in the air. I sang her a song from one of the pre-plague Human tapes, and twice again she asked me to sing it, her whole body tight with excitement—and, almost, fear. The third time I sang it she began to hum along, tonelessly at first, while Alfilere sat in her lap chewing a strip of plastic and adding his own delighted babysong.

But abruptly she broke off, glancing from side to side nervously. Wrapping her cloak of silence around her again, she signed, —This is not right! The Mother tells us that we feel—hear—the inner soul of all things. This "voice" is not from the soul, not real . . . perhaps we weren't meant to use it, or we would *know.* Her earring jingled with her desire and uncertainty.

"Etaa," I scrawled patiently, "your people did know, once; all Humans did. But after the plague they forgot how to use their voices, because no one could hear them. You've seen the Tramanian nobles move their lips, and understand each other—they've forgotten their voices too, but they remember how a mouth was used to make signs. A voice was given to every Human, so they could let people know how they felt. Think how much more you know about other creatures because you can hear their voices—feel their souls. Think how much more you'd know about people, too, if they knew how to use their voices fully!"

She stared at the message for a long time, and then she made a series of signs in Kotaane; I realized she was praying. She gathered up a handful of dust from the floor and let it drift between her fingers. At last she took a long breath, and her eyes told me before her hands did, —I will learn it.

Once she had decided, she was never silent, practicing her sounds to me or to Alfilere, or to the gliders on the warming winds of summer if no one else would listen. She immediately learned to tell one sound from another as she heard it, to my relief, and I put away my pad and stylus once I had taught her the phonemes of the pre-plague speech. Making them herself was harder, and in the beginning she answered in an earnest singsong of slurred and startling imitations, making her own translations by hand as she went along. But slowly her instinct for forming sounds sharpened; she laughed and marveled at the endless surprises hidden in her own throat. And so did I, as though together we had triumphed over ignorance and fear, and had begun to find our own private unity.

We began to spend more and more of our time together in conversation, too. She told me of her people and her life as their priestess, and about the man she loved, who had been her other half and made her whole. And that she had lost him . . . but no more than that. She kept Alfilere close in her arms as she spoke, the living symbol of her lost joy. It moved me in ways I couldn't explain, that would have made no sense to her; and somehow for the first time I began to feel the real nature of heterosexuality, and sense the kinds of love and desire that made it possible, the ties that could bind such a terrible wound of dichotomy.

I almost told her then that I had seen her husband, and that I knew he was still alive. She had asked me often for news of the king, and of the Smith, who led her people against Tramaine. When she asked about the Smith, sorrow and longing for the past made her tremble. But I thought she couldn't know that the Smith and her man were the same: that the Libs had found him broken at the bottom of the cliff and saved his life, and had used his own love and outrage to make him their tool for change. He fought for her now like a hero out of Kotaane legend . . . and he might still die for her in the end. And so, though I told her what I'd heard about the Smith and the king, to spare her further anguish I never told her what I knew.

Etaa pressed her curiosity about my nature too, as we began to feel more free with one another. Who was I? What was I? Why were we here among Humans? I was forbidden by my training to give her the answers; but I gave them to her anyway. Cut off from everything, with even my own form getting unfamiliar, this separate world I shared with Etaa and her son was suddenly more important than my own—and in a way, more real. If I had been less impulsive, or more experienced, maybe I wouldn't have become involved; but if I hadn't, this galaxy would be a different place today.

But Etaa had been open with me, and so I opened myself in return. I told her about my "home" far off among the stars, farther away than she could ever imagine—so far away that I had never even seen it; how I had been born in space, and followed my parents into the Colonial Service. I tried to tell her how many worlds there are, and of the limitless varieties of form to be found upon them, all lit by the unifying fire of life. How much of it she believed, I'll never know, but her eyes shone with the light of other suns, and she always pressed for more.

I never intended to be fully open about our purpose on her world, but I felt she had a right to know something about why she had been stolen into exile. So I told her we had come to make things comfortable for people on Earth—so that they would never want to leave it and intrude on our stars. We had helped the Tramanians to lead better lives, and if the Kotaane ever "needed" us we'd help them too. I explained to her about the starfolk faction that wanted to stir up trouble among her people (and stir up progress too, but that I didn't say): how they had encouraged the Kotaane to fight a painful, vicious war they could only lose, and caused endless suffering and misery, when the rest of us wanted only to bring peace to her Earth. But Tramaine's king had begun the war by stealing her, and so we had rescued her from him, to help stop the ill-feeling (but primarily to keep the king from raising an heir to the throne who would be hostile to us, but I didn't say that, either). Let the angry king win the battle with the Kotaane but lose the war for progress, and the Libs would suffer a policy setback it would be hard to get over.

Etaa listened, but when I finished I noticed her dark eyes fixed on me, as bright and hard as black diamonds in the firelight. She said, "If you have taken me to save me from the king, then why won't you let me go to my people? You say it would stop the war—"

I hesitated. "Because the war wouldn't stop now, Etaa. Too much else is involved. When the war is over you can go home; it's not safe for you now, while the king could still search for you." And so could the Liberals, and they would have found her.

She set her silver bell ringing softly, with fingers that were still nervous to form a reply. "I *know* why the war will not stop. You say starfolk want peace for us, and comfort, and only a few wish us trouble. Then tell me why the 'Gods' urge the Neaane to burn my people and persecute them! My people are not fools to be misled, they fight because they have good cause, and the cause is you! The Neaane were our friends until you came to them, and now they spit on us. You offer us your help, 'God.' Spare us, we've had enough of it." She caught up Alfilere, who had been placidly stuffing a rag doll into my empty boot, and stood glaring at me before she turned away to her pallet in the corner.

"You've learned to speak very well, Etaa," I said weakly.

She glanced up at me from the shadows, disappointment softening her words. "Better than you do, Tam."

I settled down in my own darkened corner, listening to the sounds of Alfilere nursing himself to sleep, and his mother's sighs. And thought about the strains on a culture when new ideas come too fast, and the need for an escape valve to ease the pressure, a catharsis . . . the Humans had needed a lot of them, in their past, and the Tramanians had needed one now, so we let them have it. We let them kill the Kotaane. It was a vicious escape, but they were vicious creatures. . . . But did that make it right? Not by our philosophy of unity; not by our standards. And we upheld those standards, or I thought we did. All life is our life, and so we do not wantonly destroy any species, no matter how repulsive or threatening it is to us. We meddle, yes, to protect ourselves. But how far should it go? What about the kharks, the wholesale destruction of so many, for the "comfort" of the Humans? The kharks were the most highly developed species indigenous to the planet. Was it right to put them so far below the Human intruders? Had the Human lust for destruction infected us too—or did this politic blindness to the philosophical ideal go on everywhere?

I hadn't been everywhere—I'd hardly been anywhere, and I'd never questioned my teachings; I'd never had cause. The Liberal faction argued for more xeno self-determination, and I couldn't see the point, because with Humans it was suicide. The Libs tampered with Human society to overthrow our settled status quo, to force the sector council to accept a "better" one, and to do it caused Human bloodshed and chaos. The Libs revolted me—but had we been more honest, or only bigger hypocrites? Suddenly there were no answers; there were only Humans who suffered and died for their "Gods," and the words "More atrocities are committed in the name of religion than for any other reason." A Human quotation. I fell asleep at last, aching with fatigue and indecision, and dreamed that I met the Human empire, come to reclaim its lost colony: a colony of the deaf and blind, living in ignorant stagnation. And with the guns of their warships trained on me the Humans said, "What have you done to our children . . . our children . . . our children . . . ?"

While Etaa went through the greatest change in her life, the evolutionary changes my body was undergoing speeded up, as though my instincts had finally become attuned to the rhythm of this new world, and my body had chosen its most suitable form. Etaa never referred to the change at first, too unsure even to ask me questions. But at last, one evening, she came to stand beside me while I played with Alfilere, now more awkward than he was, and making him bounce with sudden baby laughter. Cool, dry breezes fingered her dark hair, and she asked with lips and hands, "Must you change?"

I nodded as much as I could. "I'm committed, now."

"Why?"

"Why must I change? Because it was planned that I would, for the protection of us both on an unknown world. It helps me know what to expect." The specter of a glider struck behind my eyelids: I'd recorded that this world was too unknown, that the adaptation had left me vulnerably in-between for too long. "Or why do I change?" I opened my eyes. "Because . . . every living creature changes as its environment changes, that's called evolution; but my people have the ability to change very fast. What takes most creatures many lifetimes to do, we can do in months, instinctively—in a way, like your rainbow flies change the colors of their wings in an instant, to match a flower. We've learned to control the changes when we want to, and freeze them—but when we need to understand the system behind the form, nature has to take its own course."

"*Her* course," Etaa said mildly. "Will—will you still speak with me when you are changed?"

I smiled, and Alfilere giggled, blinking up at me with wide brown eyes. "I think so. I need my voice now."

Her smile broke apart, her speech broke down into gestures. —I wish I could change, as you do! Mother, let me change my being and start again; let me lose my memories, and . . . and my sins— She rubbed her hand across her mouth like a child, pressing back the bitter misery.

"Etaa . . ." I raised myself up, holding Alfilere. "However you changed, your mind and soul would still be the same—with all the bonds to hold you. But however you changed, you couldn't choose better than to be who you are." I remembered how I'd looked forward to my change, my hope and anticipation, and said, "If you knew the truth, I wish I didn't have to change. I—I'd rather stay Human with you." I laughed. "I never thought I'd hear that—but it's true. It's true."

She took Alfilere from me and slipped open her clingsuit as he nuzzled her in hunger. She stroked his curly head and smiled again at me, her eyes so strong with feeling that I could barely meet them. "Thank you," she said, very clearly; and I knew I had been given my reward.

The change reabsorbed and reformed my Human limbs, and I settled squatly to the ground. My skin mottled rust and gray, expansible air sacs made my leathery hide sag into whispering folds: I was becoming a glider—a creature of the air, bound to the earth by my own unsureness. To be an earthbound glider was clumsy and exasperating; it was difficult even to use a recorder for my observations, and worst of all, I itched all over with the changes, and couldn't scratch. Etaa reconciled herself with her usual determined grace; she spent her evenings singing off-key to her child while she sat beside me scratching my back with a stick, and my alien body sang with relief.

During the days I haunted the cliffs, watching the gliders swing and soar, hunting far out over the maze—or sometimes closer in. Seeing me, they would set up a moaning that started tonal vibrations in my own air sacs; they lured and cajoled . . . until at last my alien desires slipped free of my inhibitions and I threw myself from the cliff and joined them. My flaccid body ballooned as the sacs expanded and filled with air: I could fly. Battered and caressed by the wind, my elemental god, mindless with exhilaration and terror, I probed the limits of the constant sky. I was one with the wind and the cloud-shadow; without thought, with only the flow of light into darkness, time into eternal timelessness, motion to rest to motion.

At last I came back to myself and remembered my duty, and my reality. I returned to the shelter, to find the hot, rising winds had turned cold in the long shadows of evening. Etaa looked at me strangely, as if somehow she knew where I had been. For a moment I saw envy in her eyes, the envy of one who could feel the unity of all things for one who could share in it.

But as I grew apart from Etaa in one way, suddenly and unexpectedly I found that I had become much closer to her in another, more profound way: I discovered that I had become pregnant. I was very young for that, barely twice her age, and separated from my own people, everyone I cared for; there was no stimulus—and yet I was pregnant. And then I realized my stimulus had been Etaa and her laughing Alfilere. But they were aliens. There was no one here of my own people to share a birth with, no one I loved, not even a pregnant stranger. How could I bring a child into the world without conjugation, to be a part of no one but me: a solitary-child, not a child of shared love, and without namesakes or a family? I struggled alone with my despair, hiding it from Etaa behind the growing strangeness of my face, until the supply shuttle came again. But Iyohangziglepi could only report "no change" in Tramaine, and sharing my misery only seemed to deepen it in the end, as I watched the shuttle climb toward the sullen clouds and turned back alone to the ruined town.

But like all natural things, I was prepared by nature to be glad, and when finally I was ready for the first partition, my fears disappeared and astonished pride filled the void they left behind. A secret pride, which I kept hidden from Etaa as I had hidden my pain, because I didn't know what her reaction would be. She had accepted everything until now—because Human culture had not progressed to the point where "miracles" were impossible—but my protective instincts kept me silent. I only made her promise to avoid a darkened back room of our shelter, and hoped she would obey.

Not trusting her with that one secret of the differences between us, thinking that one mother of a child could not learn to understand another, was the worst thing I could ever have done. And somehow I knew it, when I heard her shriek of horror; knew it, as I struggled frantically back to the shelter from the fields: she had entered the forbidden room and found my child.

"Etaa, no!" I floundered to the doorway, wild with frustration and grief.

"Tam, hurry, help me, a beast—!"

"Etaa!" My voice broke with fury—she froze with the stick in her hand, over the formless bleeding lump of gray still quivering on the floor. Its piteous cries shrilled in the range that only I could hear, fading now as its life faded. "Etaa"—the words burned my mouth—"what have you done?"

Etaa dropped the stick and backed away from me, frightened and confused. She lifted Alfilere, crying now with his own confusion and fright, and stood staring from me to the bundle of living parts that cowered on their nest, all that remained of my half-finished child. Her lips trembled. "Hywel . . . Hywel crawled into this room. And when I came after, I found—I found—*that* creeping around him."

"Etaa, that . . . is my child."

"No!" Revulsion flared in her eyes, against the truth, or against her deed, or both.

"Yes . . ." I moved to the quivering cluster, avoiding the part that lay still and silent now, and the rest gathered close, mewing for comfort and warmth.

An anguished cry tore itself from Etaa; I looked up to see her bury her face against her own child. She sank down on the dusty floor, sobbing her desolation.

I held my little ones close, and groped for the strength, the words, to help us both. "I should have told you . . . I should have warned you. They're helpless, Etaa, they wouldn't harm your son. Among—among my people, we don't have children the way you do, all in a finished piece. We form them a part at a time, by duplicating each part of ourselves; the way I was able to grow another hand, when I needed one. Some parts serve an extra purpose, protecting the rest, that are more specialized; they might have stung him . . . but it's harmless."

She looked up at me, shaking her head, her mouth drawn too tight for words.

"I should have told you, Etaa."

"They . . ." She took a long breath. ". . . they are—yours?"

"Yes."

"But, I th-thought . . . ?"

"You thought I was a man? I am. But I'm also a woman. We don't come together with another to form a child; we form our own and choose someone we love for sharing: a part of our child for a part of theirs, after the birth."

She groaned again, softly, fighting for acceptance. "Oh, Mother, help me . . . Oh, *Tam*, what have I done to you?" She clutched Alfilere against her so hard that he squalled in protest.

I looked away. She had done what all Humans did, acted from fear, reacted with violence, inflicted pain and death blindly out of ignorance. I had been a Human once, and had despised them; but only now, after I'd lost Human form, had I really learned anything about the Human mind and spirit—and now, in the face of this most terrible act, I found I could only blame it on myself. "It—wasn't your fault. And this hurt can be mended . . . we're more fortunate than you that way. It would never have happened, if you'd known all along."

But she only sat rocking her child, the bell on her ear singing softly with her helpless grief.

Etaa spent long hours alone in the days that followed, gazing out across the sighing, broken world from the doorway of the shelter or walking the rim of the cliffs with her baby at her back. The clouds that filled the sky now were only wind clouds, dark and licked with lightning, never dripping enough moisture to settle the endless dust. The wind had grown hot and parched, shredding the clouds and sweeping the dust high into the upper air, to fade the brazen blue that sometimes broke through into this land of somber hues. She watched the sky with yearning as Midsummer's Day approached, and when it came she performed makeshift Kotaane rituals; but clouds hid the triumph of the Sun, and she left them unfinished, her eyes haunted and empty.

At dusk she came to me where I crouched in the doorway watching the luminous fantasy-face of billowing Cyclops wink behind the clouds. I heard Alfilere murmur as he slept, somewhere in the firelight behind us. She pushed a dark curl back from her eye, brushed at it irritably as it slipped down again. At last she said, "It's true, isn't it, Tam?"

"What?" I waited, knowing there was more troubling her than the secret of my child.

"What you told me: that we're not on the Earth anymore. That we're on Laa Merth? And—" she struggled to keep her voice steady "—and that little speck that you see, passing over the face of the Cyclops like a fly . . . that's the Earth? I've watched the sky, and it is different; the Cyclops is shrunken, the bands on her robe are twisted . . . everything is different here. I think it must be true."

"Yes. It's all true."

"Our legends tell how Laa Merth once had children of her own, but the Cyclops destroyed them. This must be their town, and so that must be true too."

"Yes." I wondered if there was any truth in the Kotaane myths about the source of the Human plague.

"But our legends say that the Mother is the center of all things, She is greater than all things. How can She be a speck on the face of the Cyclops!"

My throat tightened with the pain that shook her voice, and I couldn't answer.

"Tam." Her fingers reached down, scraping my rough hide. "I know nothing; it is all lost on the wind. Tell me what is true, Tam." She sank down beside me, her voice wheedling and her eyes wild. "What shall I believe in now?"

"Etaa, I—can't . . ." Her fingers convulsed on my back, telling me that I *had* to, now: that my pitiless, self-centered world had torn her world away and thrown her into the darkness of the void. Her faith was her strength against adversity, and without faith she would shatter, we would all shatter. "Etaa, the Mother is—"

"There is no Mother! Tell me the truth!"

I closed my eyes, wondering what truth was. " 'Mother' and 'Earth' . . . are the same to you, in your language, in your mind. But the Earth is also the world where you live, and a mother is what you are, and I am, a bearer of life. And those things are both still real, and wonderful. Your Earth looks very small now, but only because it's far away; like Laa Merth, in your sky at home. When you return you'll see again how large it is, and beautiful—full of everything you need for life. It's like a mother, and that will still be true. The Kotaane are very wise to call themselves the children of the Earth, and be grateful for its gifts."

"But the Cyclops is greater, and stronger."

"Greater in size. But only another world." And only a brightness behind the clouds now. "Your myths are right; it doesn't love your people—it would poison you to live on Cyclops; but the Earth is strong enough to stay out of its reach, and will always care for you. And the sun will always defy its shadow, making the Earth fertile, able to give you life. You see, you've known the truth all along, Etaa."

"But . . . the worlds are not alive . . . they do not see all, or *choose* to interfere in our lives as you do—"

"No. But really in the end they are more powerful than any of us. All our lives depend on them; even starfolk need air, and water, and food to survive. We're very mortal, just as you are. Everything we know of is mortal, even worlds . . . even suns."

"Isn't there anything else, then? Is there no God, or Goddess, to give us form?"

"We don't know."

Etaa gazed out into the growing darkness, silent, and her hands formed signs I didn't know. And then, slowly, she reached up to her ear and removed the silver bell. She dropped it into a pocket of her jacket as if it burned her fingers.

"Oh, Meron," she whispered, "how did you bear it for so long, never knowing what was true, or whether anything is, at all?"

I glanced over at her, surprised; but she only got up and went to her pallet, seeking her answer in the closeness of Alfilere. I slipped into my darkened nursery to see my own child, thinking of the sorrow we two had given to each other, and the joys. And as I lay beside my forming child, I wished there could have been a way for us to give each other the greatest gift of all.

We stayed on Laa Merth for more than a third of a Cyclopean year, nearly half a natural Human year. Bright-eyed Alfilere took wobbling steps hanging onto his mother's fingers, and my own baby, full-born now, soft and silvery and new, opened enormous eyes of shifting color to the light of the world. I marveled to think that I could have been so beautiful once, for S'elec'eca was both my child and my perfect twin.

Etaa loved "her" on sight (Humans have only gender terms reflecting their basic dichotomy, and she refused to call my baby "it"); and if it was partly out of guilt and need at the start, I saw it grow into reality, while she watched both children and I studied the world outside. She called my child "Silver," her term for S'elec'eca, the name I had chosen. She said nothing more about religion or belief, and her love for the children filled her empty days; but when she absently invoked the Mother a painful silence would fall, and her eyes would flicker and avoid me. Sometimes I noticed her touching her throat, as if in finding her voice she had eaten the bitter forbidden fruit of a Human myth far older than her own and found the cost of knowledge was far too high.

When the supply shuttle came again I slithered and slid down the hill to meet it, oblivious to everything but the chance of good news for us; Iyohangziglepi nearly stunned me, thinking I was an attacking alien beast, before I remembered to call out to the ship.

But after the initial shamefaced apologies, I finally heard the news I had been waiting for so long: the war between Tramaine and the Kotaane was over. But the Kotaane had won—and not just won concessions as the Libs had planned, but won Tramaine. The king had been killed in battle, fighting to save his people; because, thanks to our Archbishop Shappistre, the people wouldn't fight, cursing the king and expecting us to take their side when we couldn't. And so the Liberals had won too, and the Service would have to support the Kotaane; but the Kotaane didn't know what to do with their victory now that they had it. They wanted only their priestess, and their peace, and the shattered Tramanians filled them with disgust: so signed the warrior Smith. Once I would have said that he was lying or insane, or else he wasn't Human. But he was Etaa's husband, and I believed him.

But if it was true, then nothing was settled, and Etaa's world teetered on the brink of more chaos. Iyohangziglepi said bitterly that even the Libs were appalled at their success in changing the world: because of it, we were faced with leaving the Humans to worse grief than we had caused already, or interfering in their culture to a degree that would destroy all that was left of our faltering integrity. Etaa could go home at last, and so could I. But to what kind of a future?

Etaa was still waiting eagerly at the top of the hill, watching my return from the ship. She held a child in each arm, masked against the blowing sand, and I could almost see hope lighting her eyes as I scrabbled back up the gravelly hill and the shuttle stayed on the ground behind me.

"Tam, are we going home? Are we?"

"Yes!" I reached her side, puffing.

She danced with delight, so that one baby laughed and one squeaked in surprise. "It's true, it's true, little ones—"

"Etaa—"

She stopped, looking at me curiously.

"The ship will wait for us. Let's get our things, and—and I'll tell you the news. But let's get out of the wind."

We threw together our few belongings in

minutes, and then she settled with the children on the piled moss beside the ashy fire-ring. I crouched beside her, and our eyes met in the sudden realization that it was for the last time. Taking a long breath, I said, "The war is over, Etaa. Your people have beaten the Tramanians."

She shook her head, wondering. "How can it be—?"

"Your people are brave warriors. King Meron is dead, because the Tramanians wouldn't fight them anymore; they expected the Gods to—"

"The king is dead?"

I nodded, forgetting it wouldn't show. "Long live the king." I finished the Human salute as I smiled down at Alfilere, who had come over to me and was trying to climb up my face. Etaa cradled my own little rainbow-eyes in her lap, as I longed to do, and would do, soon, at last. "Your suffering has been avenged, and the suffering of your people."

"How—how did he die?"

"Struck by an arrow, in battle against your people."

A spasm crossed her face, as if she felt the arrow strike her own heart; her head drooped, her eyes closed over tears. "Oh, Meron . . ."

"Etaa," I said. "You weep for that man? When your people hate him for taking you, and defiling their Goddess? When his own people hate him for keeping you, and bringing the wrath of their Gods? Even the Gods have hated him . . . But you, who deserve to hate him more than any of us, for running your life—you weep for him?"

She only shook her head, hands pressing her eyes. "I am not what I was. And neither is the world." Her hands dropped, her eyes found my face again. "One's truth is another's lie, Tam; how can we say which is right, when it's always changing? We only know what we feel . . . that's all we ever really know."

I felt the air move softly in the cavities of my alien body and the currents of alien sensation move softly in my mind. "Yes. Yes . . . I suppose it is. Etaa, do you still want to return to your husband, and your people?"

Her breath caught. "Hywel . . . he is alive? Oh, my love, my love . . ." She picked up her curly-haired son, covering him with kisses. "Your father will be so proud! . . . I knew it must be true, I knew it!" She laughed and cried together, her face shining. "Oh, thank you, Tam, thank you. Take us to him now, please! Oh, Tam, it's been so long! Oh, Tam . . ." Her face crumpled suddenly. "Will he want me? How can he want me, how can he bear to look at me, when I betrayed him? When he jumped from the cliff to save his soul from the Neaane, and I pulled back? How can he forgive me, how can I go home again?"

"Why did you pull back?" I said softly.

"I don't know! I thought—I thought it was because of my child." She held him close, resting her head on his while he squirmed to get free. "For half a second, I drew back—and then it was too late, the soldiers . . . But how can I know? I was so afraid, how can I know it wasn't for *me*? To let him die, thinking . . ." She bit her lip. "He will never look at me!"

"But who was the coward, Etaa? Who threw himself from the cliff and left you to the Neaane? Was it you who betrayed, or Hywel?"

"No! Who says that—"

"Hywel says it. He is the Smith, Etaa, the victor in this war, and whatever the reasons that others fought, he fought for you. All he wanted was to find you, and to repay you for his wrong. He wants you brought to him, that's all he wants—but only if it's what you want, too. He cannot send you his feelings, but he sends you this, and asks you to—remember." Carefully I produced, from a pouch in my hide, the box Iyohangziglepi had given me.

She took the box from me and opened it, lifting out a silver bell formed like a flower, the mate to the one she had worn on her ear. She searched in her pockets for the one she had taken off, and laid them together in the palm of her hand. Her fist closed over them, choking off their sound; her hand trembled, and more tears squeezed out from under her lashes. But then, slowly, a smile as sweet as music grew on her face, and she pressed them to her heart.

Alfilere had drawn Silver off her lap, and they rolled together in the moss beside her, sending up a cloud of dust. Etaa's exile and sorrow were ended at last; she would return to her people, and I would return to mine. Probably we would never see each other again, and the children . . . I looked away. What sort of a life would Alfilere have, in the world we had left him? The son of the Smith, the heir to Tramaine, the strong, gifted child of Etaa, the Blessed One . . . who would have been my child too if there had been a way; who was as dear to me as my own child. The child of unity in a broken world. The child of unity—

And suddenly it was so obvious: the answer to everything had been here in my keeping, all along.

We could raise Alfilere to inherit his birthrights, and be a leader such as his people had never known—one who could give them back their rights and give us back our pride.

"Etaa?" She looked at me vaguely, still half lost in reverie. I tried to keep my voice even, not knowing if she felt the same way I did, or what her reaction would be. "You know the situation back on your Earth is very unstable right now. The Kotaane have won a war they didn't expect to win, and they don't know what to do about it. Your husband wants only to go home with you, not to rule a kingdom. Your people despise the Tramanians, and now the Tramanians despise themselves. They don't even know what to think about their Gods, they have no leadership; all the nations that surround Tramaine will be shaken, and there'll be more war and hardship that could involve your people, unless something is done—"

She frowned, and reached to catch up the escaping children.

I released air from my sacs in a sigh. "Yes, I know. *We've* done too much already. Even the Service can see that, finally. But if some new answer isn't found, some compromise, things will keep on getting worse. We could destroy you, Etaa, with our meddling, unless somehow you stop being a threat to us. And if we did that to you, we would have destroyed ourselves as well."

She shifted the babies uneasily on her knees. "You have a plan to stop it?"

"I do . . . I *think* I do. . . . When I met you, I thought all Humans were violent and cruel without reason. That's why we were afraid of you, why we wanted you to stay where you were. But now I don't believe it. Your people are more aggressive than we are, and you have to learn there are responsibilities to progress that can't be ignored; you have to grow in understanding as you grow in strength.

"But your cultures are still young, and maybe if you begin to learn now how to live with one another, when you come to us as equals between the stars you'll be able to live with us as well. The time is perfect now, in the balance of change, for a religion to show Humans the unity of all life, and how to respect it—as your people do, when they follow the teachings of the Mother. And there is the perfect sign of that unity, the perfect *Human* to begin it: your son." I shifted nervously, trembling with hope and love. "Etaa, will you give me your son? Let me raise him, among my people, and give him the chance to change your world forever."

Her eyes stabbed me with incredulity and betrayal. "My son? Why should you take my son?"

Blindly I said, "Because he's the child of the Kotaane and the child of the Neaane. Let him inherit his father's throne, and close the wound between your peoples forever."

"He is not the king's son! He is mine, and my husband's."

"Only you know that, Etaa. The Tramanians believe he's the heir to their throne."

"My husband knows. He would never agree, he would never give up his son and clan-child."

"Hywel would be proud to give his child such an honor! I know he would, I . . ." I faltered, in my terrible need to be right.

"No!" Her hand rose in a fist. "I will not! Do you think we're less than animals, that you can take our children and we'll never mind?" Her voice broke. "Tam, eight years we waited for this child—eight *years*. How can you think we could give him up?" She looked down at me, her eyes changing. "But I forget; you aren't even Human." It was the first time she had made that an insult.

And I suddenly remembered that I wasn't, that we were still two totally alien beings who would never really know each other's needs or share each other's dreams; and there would never be an answer that was right for both our peoples. "I didn't know what I was asking, Etaa. I'm sorry, I—"

"Would you give up your child, Tam?"

I saw Silver from the corner of my eye, and tiny mock hands contentedly exploring Etaa's real one. I forced my eyes to meet Etaa's. "For this, I would give up my child, Etaa. Even if it was the only child I would ever bear. If it meant the future of my people, I would. And it *can* mean the future of both our peoples."

Coldly she said, "Would you give me Silver, Tam, if I gave you my son? To raise in his place?"

"Yes . . . *yes!*" I wondered wildly what emotions showed on my glider's face. "Etaa, if you could only know how you honor me, how much it means, to share a child with you. If you knew how much I've wanted you to love my child the way I love yours—it's all I could ask; to share with you, and bind our lives together."

She searched my eyes desperately, holding the children, and the future, in her hands. At last she looked down, into the two small flower faces peering up from her lap, and asked, "Would you teach him to use his voice?"

"And write, and read; and hand-sign, too. And to respect all life, and make others want to do the same. He's a good, beautiful baby, Etaa; let him be a great man. Let him be all he can be. He could save your world."

She shook her head aimlessly and no silver song answered now to give her comfort. "Is this true? Is it the only way to help? Will it help everyone in the world?"

"It's the only way, if you want the Humans to have any say in their own future, Etaa. If you want to save yourselves from our meddling." The knowledge tore at me that I was the biggest meddler of all, not shifting the fates of anonymous aliens, but tearing apart the life of someone I knew about and cared about, who had suffered so much—for a dream that might never come true. And what if I was wrong? "Etaa—"

"All right," she said softly, not even listening. "Then it must be, if we are to have our future. If you will love my son, if my son will be all he can be; if the *world* can too, then . . . I will share my child with you." The final words fell away to nothing. But she looked up, and for a moment her voice was strong and sure. "There is no one else I would do this for, Tam. Only for you. Don't let me be wrong."

I kept my un-Human form hidden in the shuttle when we returned to Tramaine, to the town by Barys Castle where it all began. Etaa rose from her seat as the lock opened; beyond, in the darkened afternoon of early autumn, I could see the congregation of resplendent artificial gods—and goddesses, our "manifestation" of the Mother's willingness to accept this new union of beliefs. Beyond them were the milling Human representatives, and somewhere among them, a dark-haired warrior who only wanted his wife.

Etaa took Alfilere up in her arms for the last time wrapped in a royal robe, and I saw her shiver as he nuzzled her neck, cooing. Her face was the color of chalk, frozen into a mask too brittle to melt with tears. She left Silver squirming forlornly alone on the foam-cushioned seat.

"Etaa–?" I said. "Won't you share my S'elec'eca?"

In a voice like glass, she said, "I couldn't take Silver, Tam. I love her, I *do*—but how could I teach her what she was meant to be? And my people wouldn't understand her. It wouldn't be fair. I will try . . . try to help them be ready for my son. And maybe someday for Silver, too. Will you bring her to see me then?"

"I will," I said, wanting to say something else. Tears crept down my face like glue.

"Will you always be with him, and Silver too?"

"Yes, always . . . and never let him forget you." I hesitated, looking down. "Etaa, you'll have more children. And it doesn't have to be eight years again. There are ways, we can help you, if you want us to."

Her mouth stiffened in angry refusal; but then, softening, she bent her head to kiss Alfilere and said very faintly, "I would like that . . . Tam, I should hate you too, for everything you've done. But I don't. I can't. Good-bye, Tam. Take care of our children." She knelt and stroked my mottled hide, while I caressed her with the sighing hands of the wind, the only hands I had.

Etaa left the cabin, and Iyohangziglepi came to pick up Silver, who began to cry at being held in a stranger's arms. Together we watched the viewscreen as Etaa presented Alfilere to the waiting deities, with the small speech I had trained her to recite for effect. She delivered it flawlessly, standing as straight and slender as a rod of steel, and if there was any sign on her face of the agony inside her, I couldn't see it. But Archbishop Shappistre stood nearby, still tolerated by the grace of the Gods, watching with an expression that surprised and disturbed me. And then after one of the Goddesses had accepted Alfilere, Etaa turned on him with pointing finger and charged him in sign language with treason, in the name of Alfilere III and his father Meron IV before him. The archbishop turned pale, and the Gods glanced back and forth among themselves. Then one of them made a sign, and guards appeared to lead King Meron's betrayer away. Fleetingly, as if for someone beyond sight, I saw Etaa smile.

But already she was searching the Human crowd, and I saw it part for the tall dark man in Kotaane dress, the warrior known as the Smith—Etaa's husband. A fresh-puckered scar marked his cheek above the line of his beard, and he still walked with the small limp that bespoke his terrible fall. He stopped beyond the crowd's edge, across the clear space from Etaa, and his grim, bespectacled young face twisted suddenly with uncertainty and longing.

Etaa stood gazing back at him across the field, a bizarre figure in a flapping dusty jacket, her face a mirror of his own. Two strangers, the Mother's priestess who had found her voice and lost her faith, the peaceful smith who had taken heads; strangers to each other, strangers to themselves. And between them they had lost the most precious possession this crippled people knew, a new life to replace the old. The frozen moment stretched between them until I ached.

And then suddenly Etaa was running, her dark hair flashing behind her. He found her and they clung together, so lost in each other that two merged into one, as though nothing could ever come between them again.